WAITING

For Pat

Peter Asher

WAITING FOR PAT

AUSTIN MACAULEY
PUBLISHERS LTD.

A CIP catalogue record for this title is available from the British Library.

ISBN 978 1 84963 659 9

www.austinmacauley.com

First Published (2014)
Austin Macauley Publishers Ltd.
25 Canada Square
Canary Wharf
London
E14 5LB

Printed and bound in Great Britain

Acknowledgments

Thanks to Linda for guiding a dream towards a reality.

Introduction

I was two and a half when I went into hospital, during the early 1950s. For fourteen months my right leg was in traction. Like the 'hero' in these stories, I also had a poorly heart. Parents weren't allowed to stay with you in those days – just visit twice a week.

Pat was five. She fussed around me, just as she does Poorly Boy. Pat had tumours on the brain. She didn't reach six. She left her empty bed beside me one night. These stories are about Poorly Boy's fifth year. It's for the reader to decide whether he reaches six.

Poorly Boy's story is nothing like my story – other than what's on this page, and that both of us were greatly influenced by Pat. These stories are what I leave for Pat.

Peter Asher.

The Idea

Poorly Boy had not always been Poorly Boy. There was a time when he had a proper name like other boys and girls. When he was three he lost his name in the garden playing football with Ben, his father. Ben had carried the screaming child indoors. Rushing in the ambulance to hospital, the boy's heart stopped twice, maybe more.

Three weeks later, Teddy disappeared. Edward had named Poorly Boy 'Poorly Boy' and Poorly Boy cried when he went. Edward never appeared again. He may have been stolen or perhaps he was just fed up with hospitals and ran off. Sue and Ben never knew. Poorly Boy's heart was ill, and it made the child feel ill. It had once been very well indeed.

"No more football, no more fun," the doctors said. "Happens sometimes. Be like it for his life, though it could be treated. Always, however, the need to be careful."

Teddy must have wanted a well little boy, but the name Poorly Boy remained. So did the idea. Teddy's disappearance meant a lonely night in the hospital bed. Could it be that Teddy had been ill and not told anyone? Could he have gone away to a bear doctor? Do all poorly toys go away to find doctors – dog, cat, monkey, rabbit doctors? Why not just one doctor? Why not Dr Poorly Boy?

Next day on the way by wheelchair to yet another boring play area, he noticed a baby rabbit on the floor, crying his little blue ears off and his little black eyes out. Baby Kenneth became the boy's first patient and, as no one claimed him, the Nurse said Poorly Boy could look after him forever.

Baby Kenneth was very demanding of the Doctor's time. He was always first and last patient for each surgery and no one else got a look-in. The remote controlled car was tried once when its batteries were low and it felt short of energy all the while. Baby Kenneth rather bad-temperedly told it to find a garage. Poorly Boy made every allowance for the young rabbit's dependence and became like a mother to him, but where could he find a father?

Ben solved the problem. Daddy Springy came up to him in the toy shop, saying how he'd love to be Baby Kenneth's father. Poorly Boy soon came to rely on Daddy Springy's wisdom and good judgement on a whole range of both medical and non-medical matters the grown-up, light-brown rabbit knew all about. Funnily enough, Daddy Springy also always agreed with the boy – always – even when Dylon Wilkis's alligator was admitted to the Doctor's broken-bone ward, or orthopaedic ward as people doctors call it.

This alligator, named Rust for no obvious reason, had a wheel missing.

'One isn't enough to be happy on,' thought Daddy Springy on his round of the children's ward.

These rounds he went on twice daily, morning and evening, whilst held in Poorly Boy's hand. Like all the toys, Daddy Springy had very short legs and, though, like all the toys, he could walk on his own, for time and convenience Poorly Boy carried him everywhere.

Dylon Wilkis had his head way down in a comic book. When he found out Rust had gone to see Dr Poorly Boy, he was livid. When he got the Nurse to get Rust discharged from hospital, the Doctor sitting up in bed gave detailed instruction as to how to treat the new wheel.

"It is rather too large," the Doctor said, "so the alligator will be better, but lopsided when you pull him along on his lead. You'll have to be careful he doesn't fall over and hurt himself again."

The Nurse listened and repeated the instructions whilst walking Dylon Wilkis away. Dylon, controlling his anger rather well, slowly allowed Rust to get used to wobbling after him, a little unsteadily, unused to the newness of all this unexpected betterness.

Baby Kenneth hadn't liked Rust much and was pleased to see him sort of stagger off. Daddy Springy thought it time the young rabbit had some responsibility, so gave him the three wheeled remote-controlled car to comfort until it got used to being a wheel short, or the Doctor found a replacement somewhere. This is when Pat put her foot down.

A couple of years older than Poorly Boy, the bossy, huge-spectacled little girl had decided to become the young doctor's mother on his first day in hospital. She had been there most of her young life. Pat pushed him everywhere in his chair, tucked him into bed every night, washed his face, scolded him even when he wasn't naughty, kissed him as often as possible and waited outside the door when he went to the toilet. It was she who sat Poorly Boy down and explained how he couldn't be doctor to every toy.

"You can't fill beds with broken motors and sticky windmills, silly. Now you're walking about and going home soon – what's your outside mummy going to say when you bring all these bits of poorly plastic home? Be doctor to soft toys only. Keep it simple. You make soft toys better as big doctors make us better."

She delighted in calling Poorly Boy silly, but she loved him dearly as he loved her. That's why one morning a week later, before he left hospital, he was surprised to be woken by the Nurse and not his inside mum.

"Pat's had to go to her mummy," the big doctor said.

"No," replied Poorly Boy, "I think she'll have gone to God to ask if He has any poorly toys I can make well for Him. She said she maybe would."

Poorly Boy noticed tiny beads of tears in the corner of the Nurse's eyes just as he had noticed his own.

"She left Little Nelly for you to keep well for her. Said she'd come back one day to make sure you're looking after her, Poorly Boy."

Baby Kenneth, quite the young rabbit now, put a loving arm around the soft pink elephant, remarkably like him in size, and said he would personally take care of her forever. Poorly Boy could never look at Nelly without thinking of Pat and sending her his love. He always expected her to turn up at any moment, mended by the big doctor.

"So you see, Mum, I'm going to be a doctor to every poorly soft toy I can."

Sue sat, looking glum, holding Daddy Springy and Nelly as Poorly Boy told her of his life's mission and future work.

"Now I'm alone I can practise all my doctor things without nurses getting on to me and Daddy Springy."

"We'll see," said Sue.

"I know we will," said a smiling Poorly Boy. "I knew you'd agree with Daddy Springy, Pat and me."

Sue continued to look glum for a few moments, alone, thinking to herself. Baby Kenneth then came in, carrying some toast for Nelly.

Little Sheeps

Poorly Boy was puffing out his cheeks and blowing on washing-powder boxes.

"Stop it, Poorly Boy," said his mother's legs.

"Behave!" said the trolley wheels.

"Love me," said Little Sheeps.

Little Sheeps was ambushing from the thickets of sweets growing in the supermarket, and Poorly Boy was looking for poorly sheeps and broken rabbits – as broken down as Poorly Boy himself. At home were hundreds and millions (about twenty) of injured creatures, and Little Sheeps knew, and that's why Andrew Wallace had been magicked into dropping him there – to ambush Poorly Boy.

"Love me. Take me home," pleaded the slightly grubby sheep. "I'm ill and have grime disease."

Nothing threw Poorly Boy, and with one last cheek-puff he picked up the crafty sheep and pushed him into his mother's hand.

"Mum, Little Sheeps wants me to wash him. He has a dirty face and nobody loves him."

The trolley squeaked in disgust and ran over Sue's foot.

"Poorly Boy, put that back at once!" But she knew it was hopeless.

"It's not one of Lippo's 'cos it's no label, and I saw Andy Big Nose put it there."

Where? On the trolley – too late.

Poorly Boy looked even more poorly and so much more sad – and the lady supervisor wanted to take him home, and he knew it. He weaved his magic fib about finding a poorly toy and how he couldn't live without it. And she agreed, even though Lippo's Law read, 'If not claimed within seven days …'

Sue was used to this sort of thing, however. She placed Little Sheeps next to Baby Kenneth, the poorly rabbit, on the pillow.

Crumble Bee

The dye had run all over its pullover and one blond eye. One purple prong was broken and bent and one was missing. It seemed to have all eleven legs, and the twelfth that might have been (it might have been a tail) was missing, maybe.

Poorly Boy got Daddy Springy to have a closer look. The old rabbit was good at looking.

"Is it a poorly bee?" said Poorly Boy. "Is its pollen spoon snapped off? Can we save it and rescue it from the gutter?"

Daddy Springy said yes as Poorly Boy helped him back into the pushchair, together with the sodden, dirty foot-long bee.

Sue grumbled all the way home, and made the bee weep more dye inside the large plastic carrier bag pushed in the tray underneath the chair. Poorly Boy got Daddy Springy to hold on to his right hand, and keep an eye on the broken bee by dangling over the side.

Once home the bee entered Accident and Emergency, where Nurse Nelly inserted her trunk up the bee's nose to see if it had hay fever. Baby Kenneth hit it with his rattle just to see if it yelled. Daddy Springy, when asked by the bee's rescuer if it would live, said yes. Sue said it wouldn't.

Poorly Boy said, "But if it's washed?"

The bee was dying all over the kitchen floor – lots and lots of purple dye.

When Poorly Boy visited the bee in the shed some time later it was drier and looking rather happier sitting up in bed.

The old dustbin lid made a good bed; and even though the bee was still not washed, Daddy Springy had been right when he said, "Yes it will live and, yes, it can stay if it stays in the shed, and, yes, it cannot go in the washing machine."

Poorly Boy sat at the bedside and removed an old onion from underneath his bottom, and gently began to ask some gentle questions.

"Dear Crumble Bee, (the matted nylon fur was starting to flake) have you any parents or little boy we should tell?"

"None," Crumble Bee groaned, surprisingly deep and awfully sad.

"Have you a mum?"

"No."

"A queen, then?"

All the rescuer got was a series of noes.

Sue arrived to grumble again, this time about the smell.

"Onions," said Poorly Boy. "This big one bit my bum and is nasty and smells."

"It's that that wretched old toy bee."

"No it's not. Crumble Bee is getting better and he doesn't smell – only where he's bled; and Nelly is going to dress his cuts again, so you'd better go, Mum."

At the end of a hot August week, the hospital smelled dreadfully of onion-smelling, sodden-wet, dried-out, stuffed, purple, nylon bee.

Poorly Boy said to Daddy Springy, "Mum ought to do something about the onions, and Crumble Bee ought to get more fresh air."

It had been a long week. The sick bee had been a good patient but his condition gave Nurse Nelly much concern.

Lots of cuddles, despite three droppings-by-mistake, had, they all agreed, saved Crumble Bee's life. The nylon onion smell had become antibiotic sprays and oxygen-cylinder smells. Poorly Boy had many chats with his guest, learning how the bee had been made 'all wrong' at the factory and thrown out the back with piles of faulty toys. The lorry had dropped him in the rainy gutter one dark night.

"Just as well it was summer," said Poorly Boy cheerfully as Daddy Springy brought in some hot soup to spoon to Crumble Bee.

Now they went into the garden to recuperate, and Sue circled the camped nursing staff, informing them, "Still no dirty toy, dry or not, in the house."

It didn't matter. Baby Kenneth had a new friend; Nelly had someone fresh to cuddle and drop; and Daddy Springy had someone different to say yes about, so Poorly Boy could always be right. The thing was, who would give the bee a permanent home and where? And seeing as Sue was against purple bees, and he couldn't even go into the kitchen, and all soup and chocolate, bacon sandwiches and ginger biscuits (things essential to a bee's health) had to be taken in all weathers to the Garden Shed Infirmary, Poorly Boy's expert team had to find a home quickly.

It was getting darker too, as September took the trees' leaves and made long shadows and hid the sun a little earlier each evening.

It was Little Sheeps who came up with the answer. Little Sheeps had been away on summer holiday at the back of the cupboard; arriving back refreshed and thinking better, he assessed the situation at once. Sue went out with Uncle Peter every Friday. It was like a weekly holiday for her.

The toys all had their yearly holiday at the back of the cupboard. Having been in the open air so much, that nasty onion wasn't smelling Crumble Bee up so badly at all now.

Right you are then! Seeing as such a poorly, poorly bee, saved from the jaws of all those horrible funeral flowers with plastic onion-smelling pollen, would need a very long holiday, he could go where sea, sun and sand were always to be found at the back of the cupboard.

By Saturday tea, however, Crumble Bee was back off holiday, back in bed in the shed.

"Oh, a fine thing to do when my back's turned!" It seemed months since she'd been in the toy cupboard. "I just had a funny feeling … Certain look in your eyes Poorly Boy … seen it so often …" and so on.

When Poorly Boy went to visit on Sunday morning, the bee was not in bed.

"Where?"

"There," said Nelly. "Therapy," she remarked. "He's taken to gardening overnight, just like that. I've mentioned it to him before about hospital work being good for you – fresh air and onion- growing too," said the clever nurse.

"He can look after the hospital garden for us!" yelled Poorly Boy clapping his hands, dropping Nurse Nelly on her trunk.

"Official Hospital Gardener and Charge Bee" – how wonderful that the designer of the Garden Shed Infirmary had had the foresight to make each ward adaptable to onion beds, biscuit dispensaries and constant friendship operations! Poorly Boy closed the door. He'd go and congratulate the designer himself – thank him in the mirror that night.

Crumble Bee's Exciting Day

All those people! He didn't like the thought at all. Not for a moment would he have spoken to them both, for he liked to see the happiness in their eyes, which reminded him of himself when he looked in the mirror when all the world was, if not 'seaside', then 'a poorly toy made better'.

Actually Poorly Boy hated the seaside on a hot, people-swarming summer's day; but Sue and Ben loved it, he knew, so he pretended to be excited at the prospect. This pretend started the evening before, when he persuaded Daddy Springy to pretend to be excited at the prospect. Baby Kenneth, Nelly and Little Sheeps were all acting excited too, for none of them wanted to go either, strange as it seems.

In the car stuck in a jam, baking in the heat of the excited sun on its way to the seaside and streaming in through the car window, Poorly Boy and his staff bravely played 'How delighted we all are!' Or one did and one didn't.

Ben had whispered to Sue in the last minute before setting off that Crumble Bee had been grumbling to him that he never got out of looking after the hospital. Poorly Boy had informed Ben previous to this not only how excited he was, but that the others had begged him to take them too, so his entire staff was going.

"Great," not too convincingly mumbled Ben. Then Ben had gone to Sue saying, "Sue, he's taking the lot with him. That's all we need! He'll lose one of them in the crush on the sands and we'll spend all day trying to find Baby Kenneth or whoever gets lost. I've an idea that might change Poorly Boy's mind."

So Crumble Bee had complained to Ben at just the right time, and Poorly Boy had agreed that it would make a nice change for the bee.

" But he's a bit grouchy, Dad, even when he's in a good mood, so it's best we only take Daddy Springy as he won't dare fall out with him." (This was later to prove untrue.)

Ben nodded a smug sort of nod.

Poorly Boy just had time to tell the others they wouldn't be going to the seaside, and they all clapped their paws, trunks and ears and ran about quietly cheering. A bar of chocolate and some dusty peanuts (the same ones always used for similar leavings) were placed on the bed, together with some comics and a jigsaw puzzle of Hampton Court Maze, so they wouldn't get bored. As none of them were into computers – and Poorly Boy wasn't too keen either – he felt he needn't warn Little Sheeps (the eldest, so in charge) to be careful when plugging in.

Baby Kenneth sat smiling with a lap full of dusty red peanuts. Poorly Boy kissed each in turn, and within an hour or so Ben was looking for somewhere to park on an exciting stretch of crowded road along the seafront at Sandhill-on-the-Rocks. It had been a happy journey.

Crumble Bee had a blister form on his left antenna – the one that was broken when he was first found.

"It often gives him trouble, Mum."

This blister got bigger and bigger as the sun, eager to get to the seaside, sat in the window nearest to Crumble Bee and hitched a ride from this position, never moving until they had arrived.

Daddy Springy told him to move to the inside of the car, where there was lots of room on the other side of Poorly Boy, Sue was in the front next to Ben. Crumble Bee refused. His eyes were bad and it was dark further inside. His eyes would be strained and start to water.

"But it's still lighter in the car than in the shed," said Daddy Springy.

"Yes, but the shed's not moving," moaned the bee.

The original logic of this prompted Sue to ask if the bee could be shut up in a not too drastic way as he was making her feel less excited than she'd like.

"Don't worry, Mummy – Daddy Springy knows what's wrong. Give us the lotion."

"No use arguing, Mum," said Ben wearily, though she did all the while as she rummaged for the suntan lotion in her bag, which also contained personal items such as Poorly Boy's heart tablets, Ben's stomach tablets and Sue's special travel mints (the ones that soothed her nerves on journeys just like this one).

Naturally always right, by the time they got the car parked (at least 300 yards from the beach), Daddy Springy was explaining how he'd concluded that Crumble Bee had sunburn.

"Blisters," offered Poorly Boy in support of the rabbit's lecture: "you can always tell when the ear blisters."

This was far less long-winded than the rabbit's medical-type non-medical terminology.

Both Sue and Ben were feeling excitement ebb from them as the Sandhill tide ebbed. Ben was also worrying how much the long scratch down the side of his car (fault, of course, of that other car) was going to cost him. Sue was fed up and irritated with her husband and the big-headed rabbit, the small-minded bee, and, by no means least, Poorly Boy and his big imagination – herself as well for forgetting to bring another packet of those so necessary mints.

Things improved when at last they saw the beach. At least hope was renewed. They located a spot of body-less sand underneath the rusty pier, well out of the sun, which suited Crumble Bee no end. The relief of making him happy caused Sue momentarily to forget how impossible it would be to get any tan in that situation. The moment of relief soon over, Ben and Poorly Boy rapidly vanished from sight down a deep hole. Daddy Springy sat by Sue, becoming sandier and sandier as the one and a half diggers showered sand over them. It was all very exciting – especially after the hole had been dug, when they straight away filled it in again as neither of the diggers could find any use for it.

Sandwiches were exciting and the sandy grit filled ones tasted particularly good – so much so that the unexpectedly happy Crumble Bee was given them all to eat after expressing his great liking for them. Sue's tan was definitely postponed as dark clouds now began to drop rusty rain upon their heads from the pier above. The seafront café was, however, genuinely exciting. Ben got into an argument with Sue, who'd forgotten to bring his stomach tablets from the car. Daddy Springy got into an argument with Crumble Bee (most unexpectedly as well) about the rabbits envisaged extension to the Garden Shed Infirmary. This would provide Nurse Kelly with 'a proper clinic for dealing with problems like clipping the toenails of stuffed Koala bears'. (Poorly Boy had been struck by the large claws on the feet of a soft toy Koala in a shop, and his inventive mind had wondered how he might deal with such feet in the event of soft toys being admitted for minor problems – not just nail-cutting, but earwax gettings-out and broken stitches. The team had to sort such things out when Sue wouldn't.)

Crumble Bee objected strongly, regardless of the sandwiches, to proposals meaning he'd lose overall control of any part of the hospital management.

Both arguments continued on and off through fish and chips, when it stopped raining for a while. Then Daddy Spring and Crumble Bee agreed to put the matter up for a vote amongst the staff (meaning Baby Kenneth would vote alone as he was the only member without a direct interest – in not much of anything as it happened). Sue and Ben didn't agree to agree to anything. The stomach tablet was hotly contested.

"You've a pocket, Ben, when all is said and done. Why leave it all to me?"

And the business of the scratch on the car also began to come back again for a nose-in.

"You weren't even looking, Sue. You weren't even on the side it happened, so I should know."

When Poorly Boy couldn't leave without fetching some 'poorly empty shells to find something to put in at home to save them from being lonely', that was it for Sue. She went back to the car in a huff. A rather downcast Ben spent the next half-hour putting a motley collection of shells in a carrier bag.

"Aren't we glad, Dad, Crumble Bee's not been the pain we all expected?" enthused an exultant Poorly Boy. "He's not grumbled hardly at all since we arrived, and he's been reasonable over the hospital thing. It's Mum who's been the most grumbly of the four of us."

Ben maintained a strained silence.

As he stood with the final shell in his hand, there came a touch on his arm followed by softly spoken words:

"Ben, I've lost the car."

To see her again brought Ben's first smile all afternoon – though fleeting. The first excitement since the café was now upon them as they chased off across the sands towards the town.

"Follow me, this way," Ben cried.

He gave me a brief smile of relief at her touch – and the dawning realisation that the car might have been stolen, scratch and all.

Poorly Boy enjoyed such events no end as he got to ride on Ben's shoulders at a real fast pace. Sue followed on as best she could, carrying bag, bucket and spades, helped by Crumble Bee and Daddy Spring.

Baby Kenneth had the casting vote, being the only voter. Quite unexpectedly, he voted for Crumble Bee, so the proposed clinic was deferred for now.

Nelly had fallen out with the baby rabbit over the Hampton Court Maze, Poorly Boy learnt after his arrival home that night. He didn't ask why and wasn't bothered, being too tired to build a clinic the next day anyway.

Lying happily in his bed, he looked back on his day at Sandhill-on-the-Rocks. The door opened and Sue came in to kiss him goodnight.

As she turned to leave she began to chuckle.

"Oh Poorly Boy, I'll never forget Dad's face, will you? I'm pleased he saw the funny side of my forgetting where the car was, and going to the wrong car park all together!"

"Yes, Mum, I nearly rolled off his shoulders when he broke up laughing. Everybody thought we'd gone mad!"

"Go to sleep now, sweetheart."

Ben stood framed in the doorway by the passage light.

"Dad, can we find an ant's nest tomorrow?"

"Whatever for?"

"So as ants can run about those seashells. That way they'll have company all the time, just like when they had little fish in them."

"I know just the place," replied Ben with a smile.

"I'm too tired to build a clinic, Dad. That's why Baby Kenneth voted against it for now."

"Yes, son, he must be growing up to make such important decisions," yawned Ben.

"Night-night, Dad."

Daddy Springy and the toys snuggled around Poorly Boy. As he drifted off to sleep, through the bedroom window he was sure he heard Crumble Bee out in the shed singing a little song lightly. Crumble Bee, as Ben had hoped all those hours ago, had had a truly exciting day.

"Just like my dad – always thinking of others."

Poorly Boy was asleep.

The Keepers-Together

Sue hated Saturdays when her husband was away on the lorries.

Ben had been a lorry driver for as long as Poorly Boy could remember, and he was all too used to him being away for long periods.

Sue missed her husband terribly, but he loved driving and she loved him enough to allow him to get on with the work he took such pride in. Driving, next to her – more than her, she thought in her lowest alone moments – kept him happy and satisfied in his work. At least this was how Sue felt in her grumpy moods – those when she was alone.

Sometimes she went to her brother's house for company – but no longer at weekends. Simply she didn't trust her son enough for that – not any more. About six months ago, when Ben was away in the big green lorry, she'd gone to Uncle Peter's on two successive evenings. When she came home after being gone an hour on that Saturday, Poorly Boy had the kitchen floor covered with old nails from the shed.

"That's the last time you get your own way and don't come to Uncle Peter's," Sue said angrily.

"But, Mum, I'm old enough to be on my own a few seconds, and Uncle Peter's is only round the corner and I'm big enough to phone, you know."

"Poorly Boy, why are you putting nails into cottage-cheese cartons with all that good, soft, rolled-up toilet paper?"

"Daddy Springy wants to get the bent ones better by nursing them straight and things."

"Oh, I suppose he doesn't mind them being hit on their heads when they're well, then." she replied sarcastically.

"That he doesn't mind at all, because they're happy doing that sort of work, standing there to be hit with a hammer. They love that part of it. But if they get bent through not being belted properly, they are unhappy and feel no use to anyone."

Poorly Boy ate a great deal of cottage cheese. He had a habit of only eating what Daddy Springy thought good for him. The doctors didn't mind, for there was a period in hospital when they thought he'd probably never recover. It was good for everyone to see the lad tucking into the revolting stuff. There was never a shortage of cartons to be cut up, stacked, rolled, filled with sand or ladybirds, trodden on accidently or used as circular beds for poorly nails.

"They won't get un-bent by lying in bed," Sue said rather scornfully.

"Of course they won't. What we are going to do is give them some peace and rest from the cold shed. They are ill and need quiet, Mum. Then we are going to belt them straight with the hammer."

"Hit," said Sue wearily. "Don't speak crudely."

"I'm not, Mum. Daddy Springy said 'belt', so blame him. Anyway, he only ever uses proper, nice words as it's all he knows."

"If it were 'all he knows', he wouldn't use ... Oh, forget it." Sue slumped at the kitchen table on a beaten chair with a beaten wave of a beaten hand.

"Mum," – Poorly Boy took her beaten hand gently in his – "you've always said how Dad was born to drive lorries. Well, nails are born to be belted – hit – with hammers, and make things look good by holding them together, just like Dad holds us together by working for us, doing what he was born to do."

Baby Kenneth had arrived, plonked on Sue's lap in order to catch the doctorly wisdom.

"Didn't little Pat once tell you to care only for soft toys?"

"Nails aren't toys at all, Mum," said an exuberant Poorly Boy – rather scornfully, she thought. "They are keepers-together, like dads and mums."

"Should be," she felt like adding. The gloom was upon her again.

Needless to say, Daddy Springy supervised while Poorly Boy told Sue how to straighten nails without causing them undue suffering.

A couple of days later, Ben came home.

"Hurt your thumb, love?" he said with concern as he let go of his wife after some big, big hugs and squeezes.

Six months later. Sue was working about the house; Ben was at work. Their son was up to something, as usual, not far away. Sue looked back over recent events as people often do on the shore of change when the tide of happening has gone back out.

Ben and Pee Bee (his name for Poorly Boy) had set about 'fulfilling', as Ben had put it, all the well-again nails. Daddy Springy had explained his philosophy of keepers-together, and Ben there and then, with two weeks' holiday, had set about giving the nails something to live for, fit and active and raring to go as they now were. Sue wasn't asked how she'd like to spend the holiday or what suggestions she might have for giving the nails purpose.

They made a garden table with three unpainted chairs ("for keeping together when it's not raining," said Poorly Boy); a box with a lid, also unpainted ("for keeping Mum's jewels – or rather earrings – in together") and a tree house, unpainted of course, which only cats used, as it happened ("for keeping cats together"). Also, they kept shoes together in a rack and books together in a case, unpainted. Ben was happy, Poorly Boy and Daddy Spring were delighted, and every single nail had fulfilled its life purpose.

"I can understand your feelings, Sue," said Uncle Peter. "You've got to remember Poorly Boy's unusual situation and his relationship with his dad, who he doesn't see very often."

"But all of this of happiness and fulfilment never seems to include me."

"It does though," her brother replied mysteriously.

Nurse Kelly came in carrying a dirty length of tiger's tail.

"Poorly Boy, what's that filthy thing doing in here? Get rid of it at once!"

"Can't, Mum. It's for when we get a tiger to make better – or a lion or a pussy cat, 'cos it would do for any of them as well."

"Shed!" she yelled. "The shed! Give it to Crumble Bee!"

"Good idea, Mum. He'll save it in that bottle he's got full of body bits. He's got some eyes and a foot in there right now, but no tails. He'll be real pleased."

"Don't say 'happy' or I'll scream," she said under her breath.

"Leave him to it, Susan. Ben asked me to give you this. Do it, he said, when I'm gone a day or two."

As Uncle Peter moved to the side she noticed, on the dresser behind, a simple, crude-looking letter rack that Uncle Peter must have brought from home. It was obviously a keepers-together job, unpainted too.

"Open the letter"

It was open. She read the contents. It was confirmation of a job – her husband's new job in town as a mechanic at Rutherford's, the hauliers.

"He wanted to make you happy. He wanted to be near you, Sue. He's working his final trip on the lorries and starts when he gets home."

As Uncle Peter finished, a little voice over in the door way added, "He's a keeper-together is Dad, Mum. Daddy Springy made him one; so, being one of us, he wanted to make you happy like the nails,"

She smiled to herself as she opened the microwave door. Ben would be home soon. Funny how nails could bring people together – yet we are still alone in our days at work, days at home.

"Mum, Little Sheeps upset Felix just now by kicking his milk over again coming in the back door."

"Don't worry – we'll make him happy and give him some more."

Ideally the three of them would be together all of the time.

"Or would it be that indeed?" she wondered. "How easy is it to bend a nail?"

"Poorly Boy, the microwave door. Baby Kenneth is not doing his job properly."

She'd talk to her husband that night – really talk – find out if he was happy to be at Rutherford's.

The Berlin Road Disaster

You'd never have guessed it – not from the sun's April smile or the birds busily designing spring's first nests, and not from Naomi Phillips bossing two important dolls into their red pram, and not from Poorly Boy helping Crumble Bee on with his butcher's apron ready for a day's work in the Garden Shed Infirmary. What wouldn't you have guessed amidst the ordinary orderliness of this bright, gentle morning? That day there was going to be a disaster.

Jennifer had far too many cuddly toys, according to her mother. She was fed up with having to wait whenever they went anywhere for her daughter to choose and re-choose who was going with them. At 8.40 a.m. it was four assorted bears and a duck; by nine o'clock the bears had become six teddy bears and a mole (the duck was still a duck) and they were all on board the blue pushchair, proceeding down Porter Road.

Porter Road (named after Cole) and Berlin Road (after Irving) met as if to shake flagstones in friendship at a place where a very high fence hid what must have been a shy (though big) house and garden. The fence was so high that neither road could see the other until they met joyously on this corner.

Mrs Wallace was late for the dentist, whilst her daughter Jennifer was rushing ahead, explaining this to the concerned passengers. Naomi was late for a chocolate bar at her grandmother's, it all being the fault of her two teenage dolls, who took far too long putting on make-up to go out. These teenagers on Berlin Road had no idea of the duck and bears worrying their way in haste down Porter Road, but all parties were nevertheless converging at speed upon the blind corner.

Nurse Nelly did not like having her trunk tied in a bow, and a heated argument had developed during the ten minutes since Poorly Boy had accidentally caught her trunk in the bow of the butcher's apron.

"You oughtn't to be wearing the theatre gown in bed anyway," she snapped at Crumble Bee. "And I know for a fact that patients don't like you doing operations in a butcher's apron. You look like a big striped pudding, not a doctor at all," she added hurtfully.

"If you continue to argue with your superior, Nurse Nelly, I'll have your sweetie allowance halved this week," threatened the eminent surgeon, who had already come a long way since Poorly Boy had rescued him, literally from the gutter. He did, however, look rather silly in the red-striped apron Sue had been pestered into making. "Go and attend to Geoffrey Koala's bottom-wiping this instant!"

"Oh, go and do it yourself if you're so superior," retorted Nelly, and with that she punched Crumble Bee on his ragged yellow nose. It was 8.15 a.m.

Poorly Boy was bored. It was Sue's washday, and Ben was away long-distance lorry driving. Uncle Peter was doing his garden – it being spring, he'd said. Worst of all, nobody was ill in the Garden Shed Infirmary, other than Geoffrey with diarrhoea, and of course Crumble Bee with a sore nose.

"Oh I wish someone would get sick," sighed Poorly Boy, going into the house with Nelly, who was still smarting at her encounter with the surgeon. "Let's find Daddy Springy and have a geography lesson. No, better still, let's go and paint the ambulance."

He'd had this idea in mind for a while – turning his red plastic wheelbarrow into an ambulance simply by painting it. Poorly Boy's bright eyes lit up at the idea as the switch of his imagination clicked to 'power on'.

"I'll black it, as black's all we've got. Come on Nelly – let's fetch the others."

They found Baby Kenneth brushing his tooth, and brought Daddy Springy and Little Sheeps out of the living room, where they'd been studiously reading a world atlas (probably bigger than the world) on the sofa. The elder brown rabbit – the real boss of the organisation – agreed that lessons could be done later, after the essential 'blacking of the ambulance'.

By 8.50 a.m. it had a neat-ish black nose on one side with two matching eyes on the other. A black smiling mouth up front completed the livery. Poorly Boy's tiniest of tiny watercolour brushes were ill fitted for the major paint job of all over.

Poorly Boy was about to remove black splashes from himself, Baby Kenneth, Nurse Nelly, Little Sheeps and Crumble Bee's now black bleeding nose (the bee no doubt regretted coming to find his nurse in order to ask her if she'd have her job back with an increased sweetie allowance). Suddenly a terrible scream followed by a horrible sight attacked the team's senses.

Naomi Phillips stood inside the garden gate, if not screaming, then enthusiastically whimpering. Her knee was only just bleeding, a bit. The real horrific sight came a moment later when Mrs Wallace arrived, holding the leg of a real plastic teenager.

Sue came out to hang clothes as if on cue. What met her looked oddly frozen in time. Her immediate attention focused upon Poorly Boy.

"That's the second perfectly good brush you've ruined this week. Well, I warned you you'd be for it if you did it to another. They're too small for sheds and ambulances, you naughty boy."

During the execution of these three sentences, she'd noted her son's increasing speed of movement in a forwards direction, past the standing figures by the gate, into the road and out of sight in the direction of the corner. No sooner had he gone behind the hedge than he reappeared and ran back to her, smiled, shoved the team into the ambulance, and ran away at high speed once more, past the still figures, off towards the corner.

Uncle Peter's voice was heard somewhere in that direction. He appeared next, out of the hedge, together with Jennifer, who, ignoring her mother, ran up the path towards the old shed.

"I've got to get the beds ready in casualty," Poorly Boy's mother thought she said.

Things were happening either very fast, very slow, or maybe not at all.

"Hello, Sue," said Uncle Peter cheerily to his sister. "You look a bit pale. Not very good today?" Before Sue could reply, Uncle Peter continued: "Just met Poorly Boy. Lost Baby Kenneth. Flew out of the ambulance, him and Crumble Bee. Would have got to the accident without either had it not been for me shouting and catching him up. You know the girls and Mrs Wallace, don't you? Live near me in Porter Road."

Sue did. Jennifer and Poorly Boy had sometimes played together. What she didn't know was what was happening. From here on, things really got confused.

Later her clearest recollection was of Uncle Peter vanishing after Poorly Boy, this time calling back that he'd have to bring the wreckage in and help Poorly Boy with the bodies. She also recalled that Sandra Wallace asked to use the phone to cancel her dentist. Yes, and could Naomi call her grandmother? Sue had muttered that she'd use the phone herself, given the chance, to call for a doctor's appointment as soon as possible. She felt poorly.

"What's going on?" she hollered as Uncle Peter neared the gate, his eyes fixed on Mrs Wallace. "Peter, what are you idiots playing at?"

"Nothing," he said in a hurt tone whilst walking back to her. "Here hold this."

It was a one-legged teenage doll from Jennifer's mother's other hand.

"Won't be long," he added, and with that he was gone.

"Any dead, Poorly Boy?"

"No, Uncle – lots of shaken and bruised teddies and a sprained duck. He was lying in the road as me and the team got near, and I saw him get run over and beak – brokened. The car didn't even slow down. Just in time, though, we were. Rescued him from a bus at the stop on Porter Road. 'Nother minute and he'd be under it and finished. Done for!" added a reflective Poorly Boy.

"Done for!" Another howl came from Sue. "Peter, stop encouraging him!"

"Shush!"

Sue was speechless with shock at this from her younger brother.

"How will you treat him?"

"Don't need to, Uncle Peter – he's a rubber duck."

"Is Vicky alright?" Naomi, returning from phoning, enquired after her doll.

"If she's the one with one leg, no" replied Poorly Boy. "I've stopped the blood with chewing gum till Crumble Bee insults her."

"Consults," corrected Uncle Peter, chuckling, but trying hard not to.

"No, she's the other one; Francesca," informed Naomi patiently.

"Vicky's just lost her hair, that's all." Poorly Boy smiled reassuringly.

Sue helped the weeping Naomi inside the house.

It was as well those with faint hearts and nervous dispositions left the scene. The Garden Shed Infirmary had fifteen beds and two cottage-cheese cartons. The beds were of the cardboard-box type for easy cleaning and removal. The cottage-cheese pots were of the plastic, squashable sort for when anyone walked over one by accident – preferably when no patients were in, though this couldn't always be guaranteed. Most of these now container traumatised teddies, a bandaged mole, a very healthy rubber duck (considering), and a one legged teenage girl.

Jennifer, a brave and non-squeamish child, was pluckily assisting Nurse Nelly to bandage limbs and paws and beaks and to change blood-stained toilet-roll bedding.

The blood was to indulge Baby Kenneth, who liked lots of it around, whether there were patients there or not. Today, of course, there was gallons of blood. The young and tender baby blue rabbit was right now under the direction of Daddy Springy, comforting the sick and asking them if they'd noticed all the blood there was about. Little Sheeps was doing as little as possible, performing his always preferred role – if he could get it, which he usually could – of Mr Crumble Bee's personal secretary. Little Sheeps was just a bit lazy and as Crumble Bee was a bee of few words (and fewer worthwhile thoughts, according to Nelly) the secretary's job didn't even need a pen.

The eminent surgeon himself, still resplendent in butcher's apron (which, as baby Kenneth was pointing out to patients, was covered in blood, both sides), right at this moment was handing out chocolate buttons to keep his colleague's energy levels up whilst throwing out unwanted bits of anatomy a moment later (or even the same moment) with the same hand. The other was turning Geoffrey Koala out of bed to put Vicky in instead.

"Look at Francesca's stuck-on leg, Naomi. A Crumble Bee speciality, it is," said a beaming Poorly Boy.

"Chewing-gum grafting, it's called. Invented the treatment himself after Daddy Springy had a tooth come out he didn't want to lose. Your dad can glue it on if it falls off. The treatments not perfect yet – needs working on. Vicky's hair can be cotton wool your mum paints and glues in place, maybe with the same glue your dad uses for the legs. She can borrow it off him."

Naomi Phillips scowled, swiped Little Sheeps out of the way, grabbed her dolls and indignantly walked off, putting her tongue out at Poorly Boy as she went.

Sue came in with Mrs Wallace.

"Ready for home, Jennifer? Pete's fixed both your pushchair and Naomi's pram. She just passed us looking rather hostile, I thought."

"She's bothered about her bald doll. Too much excitement, that's the trouble," replied Poorly Boy drily and sagely.

That evening, with only two teddies and the duck (which Poorly Boy had taken to greatly and intended swapping with Jennifer if he could) detained overnight for observation, Sue sat alone watching TV. Poorly Boy was asleep upstairs. There were three more days before Ben would be home.

"Hope tomorrow's less hectic than today," she mused. "What was it Peter called it earlier on the phone? 'The Berlin Road Disaster'. Typical thoughtless men! The only disaster was my washing that somebody got paint on while pushing past with a loaded ambulance."

Upstairs Poorly Boy lay cuddling Daddy Springy, debating the day's happenings. Nelly and Baby Kenneth were with the master surgeon – fast asleep, looking after their guests just to be sure they didn't develop homesickness overnight.

"Daddy Springy," yawned Poorly Boy, "you always said plastic wasn't as nice as fur, and today just shows how right you are. I'll just bet that ungrateful Naomi wouldn't thank us, though, if we bought her a furry teenage doll. Oh no, she wouldn't. She's not like that. She's not going to own up. Plastic's hard and cold, but fur cuddles and loves you back all the time – like you and me right now. But it's our work to save them and to make them better – plastic or furry, and real dogs, cats, fish and humans if we have to."

They were silent for a minute, struck by the gravity of their mission.

"Daddy Springy," – he yawned again- "why have daddies got to go to work?"

Daddy Springy had fallen asleep. The time, after all, was bedtime.

Conkering

Poorly Boy had flu. The Doctor came and told Daddy Springy how to treat him and how often to give the medicine and tablets.

"Don't allow him to go out, Nelly," said the older rabbit – loudly, so Sue could hear.

"He won't do as he's told, because he never does," Sue added to this. "If he gives you problems, get me and we'll sort him out between us," she instructed Nelly.

"I'm off with Daddy Springy in the car." Ben called in to collect the rabbit from the bedroom. "We'll see you later."

Sometimes Ben took Poorly Boy's friends out with him. Originally it had been Poorly Boy's idea, so they could see more of the world. It was not unknown for each in turn to go with him on his long lorry journeys.

Poorly Boy should have been going too, and Baby Kenneth, and Nelly, though Little Sheeps was busy helping Crumble Bee in the Garden Shed Infirmary. All three emergency beds were being tidied up, as was a bucket used for a toilet by the patients. There were no patients in at the moment.

The conker trip had been planned a week now, ever since Poorly Boy walking with Ben had seen several boys with shiny, brown horse chestnuts, just the colour of shiny brown horses.

Ben had remarked, "I'll take you and your mates on a conker-getting trip at the weekend."

"Please, Daddy – but they're not my friends; they are my staff," corrected Poorly Boy.

Now, however, the poor lad was down with what seemed like many runny noses, at least two runny eyes and lots more even than usual runny words, as he moaned on with a hot, flushed face about Nelly. She was sitting on him, it seemed – not letting him move about the house unless to the toilet.

"Stop moaning," snapped Sue, not at all sympathetically, "or I'll have the Crumble Bee collect you for the shed – and then you'll have a bucket to use. At least here you're indoors and warm. Think about all the cold animals in the woods. And what about the soft toys in pushchairs, out in this weather with their boys and girls?"

Poorly Boy had been dreaming of sneaking off, but really felt a little too unwell to try it. Now his eyes got twice as big, and twice as deep, and twice as dry at the mention of this last tragic fact concerning the plight of soft toys.

"Oh, Mummy, look – here come sunbeams to show me where they all are."

Sadly for Sue the sun was against her.

"Can I wrap up warm and go out with you? We can see if we can help some freezing zebras and hedgehogs in their pushchairs."

"No, we cannot. You've got a temperature and you're going nowhere. Nelly, sit on him harder," commanded Sue.

Sue then went downstairs to make some soup – vegetable, Poorly Boy's favourite whenever he was feeling sorry for himself.

It was not that it had been difficult persuading Nelly to go quietly down to the hall whilst Sue was busy, and it was not that the so small elephant had problems helping Poorly Boy on with his coat; it was just that she felt a bit guilty over not doing as Sue had required.

"Don't worry, Nelly. We aren't going far and the sun's out and it's a beautiful day, and the mist's only very light."

Poorly Boy felt snug and warm in his Puffa jacket, with the red scarf keeping the path warm more than his neck and getting damp as it trailed behind him like a tail.

Out of the sunlit mist came a looming pushchair shape with a shape just like Justin on board.

"Hello Poorly Boy," said young Justin's mother. "Where are you off to this bright morning?" She had a nice smile and breath came out around her words.

"Is that penguin wearing enough clothes, Mrs Frith? He looks a bit uncomfortable being dragged along in the wet grass. Can Justin get his arm back in the chair and the penguin under the top blanket, before he's poorly?"

"I'm sure he can, Poorly Boy. Pengi is nearly as wet as your poor scarf."

Poorly Boy bent over and helped Pengi and Justin's arm back in the chair and under the blanket, until just a long, soft, yellow beak and two gleaming eyes looked gratefully at the poorly doctor. Justin looked pleased too.

"Right now! There we are! One saved penguin and one sound scarf! Almost, anyway. Hope your mum likes washing, Poorly Boy. It's very dirty and you've got some of the mud on your nice silver coat."

Nelly had a bag of sweets in Poorly Boy's pocket and handed them round. Justin's teeth weren't all that expert at sticky toffee, so he kept taking it out of his mouth so that Pengi could have a chew to help soften it, whilst Nelly gave advice to the child on how to prevent penguins getting cold in winter.

"Shouldn't you be going home soon?"

"Will soon after I've found Dad. We are conkering together."

They said, "Cheers!" to Mrs Frith, who stood looking on as they travelled into the light October mist. Around the corner in the park were the many long arms of the horse-chestnut trees, all dangling their spiky green cases, but no Ben! Poorly Boy hadn't really expected to find him here at all; he'd only *hoped*. Ben and Daddy Springy would have finished shopping long ago.

"Oh, if only I hadn't got flu!" snapped Poorly Boy. "You should have had it instead, Nelly," he said rather ungraciously. Then he kissed her and said sorry.

They were both feeling the cold by now, so they headed for home, but not before Poorly Boy found two small and undernourished conkers begging to be picked up and carried in a warm pocket. Slowly, and a little uneasily, they made their way back. There would be a big telling-off awaiting them, for certain.

"Bet you'll be in more trouble than me though," Poorly Boy said cheerfully. "You were supposed to keep me in, Nurse Nelly.

Indeed she was in trouble. Poorly Boy was wrong, however, in thinking she would be in more of it than him. They met Sue, angry and upset, in the road near the road where they lived.

Not wishing to worry you about Poorly Boy's and Nelly's telling-off, let me just say he was very pleased to be in bed again. By now it was darker and the car was heard coming home too for a good night's sleep in the garage.

When Ben had counted all the conkers from the row of trees outside the town, he sat on the bed and got Little Sheeps (long since finished helping in the shed) to explain how the ancient game was played. Poorly Boy, propped up on the pillow, listened, fascinated. Ben said that when he was a lad the school yards were a sea of broken conkers, with children wading through.

"It's not allowed now, Dad, because of all the mess and cruelty."

"Eh?" said Ben.

"Cruel, Dad. Gives them headaches and their heads split open with the bruises."

"Who – the teachers and caretakers who have to sweep up?"

"No, the conkers, silly!"

Poorly Boy was forgiven by Sue. He always was and always would be. When he was well, Crumble Bee stood at the Garden Shed Infirmary door awaiting his new patients. There were fifty of them placed in dry sand in a cat-litter tray Ben borrowed from Felix, who hadn't needed it for years anyway. Some of the conkers (including Poorly Boy's two) got mould and required regular polishing with a cloth. When they were all better, which Baby Kenneth told Sue meant 'shining enough', Daddy Springy discharged them for Ben to put on the right track for a happy and healthy life. He planted them all around the garden. Daddy Springy and Poorly Boy looked on, with hands clasped in delight.

"Will they have trees for Christmas, Dad?"

Ben chuckled all the way back along the path. Poorly Boy stayed outside a while longer, to watch them grow.

The Fat Mouse

It's a little-known fact that animals and soft toys, when given the chance, will talk together. Poorly Boy had known dogs and cats to converse for hours with cuddly prawns and soft giraffes on all manner of philosophical subjects, as well as mundane ones like the raising of kittens or the loosening of stitches.

There was the matter over Jennifer's hedgehog, initially admitted to the Garden Shed Infirmary with sneezes and running nose – a suspected cold. Even with the intensive nursing skills of Nurse Nelly, and Poorly Boy himself taking a personal interesting the welfare of a friend's friend as it were, there was no improvement in Michael's condition. His soft nylon underfur got wetter and wetter with the tears of his discomfort and the sweating of his fever.

"He's not going to die, is he, Mr Crumble Bee?" whispered Poorly Boy over in the corner away from the hedgehog's hearing.

Mr Crumble Bee, self-styled 'Surgeon of the Purple Sting' frowned on in silence, looking at the floor for the answer to come and attach itself to his antenna. The floor remained blank, so the idea came to him to answer no.

"We've such faith in you dear doctor – you always know just what to do," was Poorly Boy's relieved response. "What's he got then?"

The floor was of no further help, so the two made their way over to Nelly, who, luckily for Crumble Bee, beckoned them to her with her trunk.

"His prickles are falling out."

And sure enough they were coming away in handfuls, as Poorly Boy found when he gently raised a handful instead of Michael, whom he'd gently tried to raise.

"Oh dear!" he exclaimed, wide-eyed in awe. "What'll we tell Jennifer? What'll we do?"

"We could stop putting a hot-water bottle under him," suggested Nelly.

"And you could stop washing his back in soapy water three times a day," suggested Little Sheeps, who had been studying these goings-on from the cardboard box three empty beds away from Michael, where he was resting.

"You're alive then?" said Nelly darkly.

Little Sheeps ignored the hurtful aside, obviously meant to infer he was lazy, and continued his analysis of the situation:

"It's obvious if you think about it. By trying to get his temperature down by keeping him cool -"

"Clean at the same time," interrupted Nelly indignantly. "That's why the soapy water. Mustn't forget hygiene!"

"Quite!" Little Sheeps' irritation was apparent. He resumed, "You've damped his glue, and it's not sticky any more. Same thing underneath with the hot-water bottle. Then his spines fall out. Same with his underfur, wouldn't surprise me."

"I told you I'd checked it. Why is it you always distrust me with keys whenever we go anywhere, Sue?"

Sue was a little rattled – not really mad as such, just gently seething. She wanted someone to pay for the idiocy of what they were doing right then – and it might as well be Ben.

"Because you won't deny that you -"

"Oh, I knew it! For the rest of my life I am sentenced to serve for having once – *once*, mind, in fifteen years of married bliss – forgotten to lock the garden shed – not the house, mind, the [and here he used a swear word] shed."

Driving along, Sue scolded Ben for swearing in front of Poorly Boy. Poorly Boy, having been preoccupied thus far with getting the team comfortably seated next to Ben on the ledge over the steering wheel, asked his mother if she would stop getting at his father and hold Baby Kenneth as he felt sick and wanted singing to.

"Why can't you sing to him?" she enquired indignantly.

"Because Poorly Boy's busy looking for hedgehogs with me and the team, that's why," jumped in Ben triumphantly.

It was Daddy Springy who came up with the 'real live hedgehog' idea.

"We should find one, my boy; ask it how to treat poor Michael. We can talk to the animals, can we not? I would venture further that we should allow Baby Kenneth some responsibility in this interview, as he reads a lot for his age and is versed in hedgehog lore."

"Can we go after tea to the common and get one to talk to us, Mum 'n' Dad?" Poorly Boy, dancing round, pleaded. "Everyone likes the idea and wants to go with Daddy Springy and me."

'Everyone but us', Ben and Sue communicated silently to one another in the language of glances and grimaces parents have.

"So you went to Daddy Springy after you noticed Michael's spines coming off, right, son?" Ben pieced together the story so far as they drove along.

"That's it Dad. This afternoon we all got worried and someone said let's go and ask the boss."

"And Daddy Springy is boss, as we all know well enough," commented a flat voice from a dark corner of the rear seat.

"Yes, Mum, we do," Poorly Boy agreed enthusiastically.

Upon arrival at the common, they parked, taking the ambulance (converted plastic barrow) from the car boot. It was a lovely midsummer evening. The common was packed with people and vibrant with traffic horns.

"We'll never find hedgehogs here." Ben looked around distastefully.

Sue had fallen asleep serenading Baby Kenneth in the car.

"Yes, we will, Dad. I've got some cornflakes."

"With milk and sugar?" Ben enquired.

"No, silly! With a slice of bread," corrected Poorly Boy, a little contemptuous of such ignorance.

"Who provided you with this arcane knowledge?" Ben was curious to know.

"Kenneth," came the answer.

"Not that same Baby Kenneth Mum's been singing to in the car?"

"Him," confirmed Poorly Boy. "He reads a lot of nature books, Dad, and for such a young rabbit he's clever."

"Have you got the bread?" Ben sighed.

"Mum has in her bag."

After waking Sue and safely harnessing the team into the ambulance (elastic bands around their feet held them against a piece of two-inch wood that lay end to end the same length as the ambulance so it wedged and stayed put), they set off on foot for a deserted field some way off the family-populated common.

Apparently Baby Kenneth had read how the modern hedgehog will prowl the rear of supermarkets at night opening unsold cornflake packets that have been thrown out.

"What did they do before cornflakes?" Ben, fascinated by this information, wanted to know.

"Starved," suggested Sue from the rear of the procession led by Daddy Springy at the head of the two-inch wood.

"No, they ate milk and eggs," Poorly Boy corrected her.

"No bacon then, son?" laughed Ben.

"You're not believing Baby Kenneth, Dad! You know how easily upset he is," scolded Poorly Boy.

"I know something for a fact too," interjected Sue, warming to the subject. "Milk and eggs are very *bad* for hedgehogs. That's well known."

"And that's why they changed to cornflakes and bread, Mum," exulted Poorly Boy.

At about this point they reached the field, silent but for the distant song of traffic, singing slightly louder than the unseen birds. They placed a bowl of dry, unsweetened cornflakes near a bush edging the large field, with the bread a few yards further in.

"Now what?" Ben looked upwards, frowning as the light began to fail and the evening grew colder.

"Coat on, Poorly Boy, or we're going home."

Without making a fuss, Poorly Boy did as Sue ordered, having no intention of being made to go home yet.

Poorly Boy's big brown eyes beamed into his father's.

"We wait, Daddy." His wide grin was somewhere between a disarming smile and an apology.

Half an hour later Sue took Nelly back to the car on the cunning pretext it was too dark for young female elephants.

"And youngish wives," muttered Ben, watching them go.

"Don't worry Dad. Here comes a hedgehog right now – look!"

Sure enough the grass was parting at a fairish pace ahead as the unmistakable brown, spiky bulk wobbled and shook towards them. It stopped, sensing their presence, and sniffed the unusual smells of Poorly Boy and Ben, plus the team minus Nelly.

"Kenneth," whispered Poorly Boy, "go and talk to him. Show him where the cornflakes are."

"But he's already walked past the bread and bowl without taking the least notice," observed Ben.

"He says he's not hungry, Dad."

"Who does?"

"Baby Kenneth does, Dad. Now he's telling the hedgehog about Michael," Poorly Boy added, holding the baby blue rabbit at arm's length on the ground. "He's giving us the treatment, Dad."

"I just bet he is," chuckled Ben softly.

"He's beautiful. Just look at the way his prickles shine and his eyes glisten."

True, Michael's black eyes did catch the following afternoon's sun through the Garden Shed infirmary window. Jennifer continued to sing the praises of the transformed hedgehog.

"How'd you do it, Poorly Boy?" She excitedly turned to the creature's saviour. "How'd you get him to grow another eye overnight when he'd just the one for almost as long as I've had him?"

"Not growed, Jennifer," he corrected. "Mr Crumble Bee, following Baby Kenneth's expert knowledge of real and cuddly hedgehogs, operated on his eye and ..." Poorly Boy faltered for a moment, seemingly uncharacteristically unsure of himself. Surely this was owing to no more than some passing distraction – a bird, say, sounding like a motor car. "Er, they did a very difficult and special eye-matching graft."

"Oh, really! What did they graft it off, I wonder?" bowled the amazed and impressed Jennifer Wallace right at Poorly Boy's wicket.

"The real hedgehog Baby Kenneth personally got the techniques off on the common swore Kenneth to absolute secrecy, allowing him permission to tell only the surgeon concerned – Mr Crumble Bee, in this case. I know, for I was there," declared Sue proudly, standing in the open doorway, sunlight framing her – a vision like the vision of Joan of Arc, or St Sue.

"And is it the common where you found the fat mouse over there in that bed?" Jennifer pointed.

"Em, er, yes." Poorly Boy replied, his loss of concentration behind him – perhaps behind him, where, in the doorway, with the expression of the Cheshire Cat upon her face, his mother stood. She was hardly like St Susan of the Knitted Warmer as she realised she'd have to become, as the 'mouse', unaccustomed to being without a thick prickly overcoat, would need something to keep him warm.

Ben, actually, had told Sue all that took place after she had returned to the car with Nelly: the real hedgehog had suggested to Baby Kenneth that maybe a toyshop with some cuddly hedgehogs for sale could be the best course of treatment for Michael.

"The mouse is far too fat. No wonder it's ill." Jennifer had not hidden her obvious distaste. "It's only got one eye too. No wonder! I bet it was that fat it walked into something."

"Yes," said Poorly Boy, glancing lovingly at his mother.

The Cows and the Bees

Poorly Boy couldn't reach the tap, so in that silent language he often used to talk to his friends he asked Nelly to get him a drink, sitting her on the wet draining board to assist her in this.

He'd been a nuisance all morning.

"Poorly Boy, you've been a nuisance all morning," said Sue emphatically – still patient under the circumstances.

Sue realised what long days they were for a five-year-old too ill to go to school – and what long hours for her with him under her feet!

"Nelly's bum's wet, Mum. Isn't she silly sitting in the silver water."

"No Poorly Boy, she's doing what you told her, I suspect. And getting you a drink isn't as important for its nuisance value as getting her bottom wet by sitting her on the soaking drainer, is it?"

Sue with Nelly in one hand and clothes pegs in the other, was going into the yard. Nelly waved her trunk and feet at Poorly Boy from the washing line, where she seemed to be enjoying herself swinging to and fro. He pulled faces at her through the kitchen window while standing on the chair he shouldn't stand on but might as well, Sue's back being turned to him at the far end of the garden.

He was just about to split his chin open; the chair tilted at that angle chairs enjoy splitting chins open at. Instead, the chair stopped what it was planning at the precise moment Poorly Boy's tongue stopped full length away from his face, facing Nelly. Poorly Boy's eyes were almost as far away from his face as the tip of his tongue.

A vision of blue- and-white loveliness had appeared on top of the fence between his garden and next door's. Sue had seen it too and was only prevented from reaching it first, being just a few steps away from the fence, by having to pick Poorly Boy up. He had tripped over in his haste to get to the vision first.

"It's Buttercup, and she's for the church fête tomorrow, so don't you go trying to beg her off me," Joan warned Poorly Boy, passing the soft toy to Sue to hand down to him. "You've had too many of my little ones already one time or another," continued the old lady next door, who was a specialist at handicrafts, including occasional cuddly toys for church events and good causes.

Many of these good causes had been called Poorly Boy, who in turn had passed them on to children he'd made his own good causes while out shopping downtown. Sue at first had tried stopping him, saying how Joan wouldn't like him giving toys away she'd given him. Poorly Boy pointed out that Father Christmas gave all his toys away as a boy and went on doing it even now as an old man. Sue had given up telling him it was Father Christmas's job, when poorly Boy replied simply that it was his job too, since Father Christmas, Jesus, Pat and the rest of them had saved his life in hospital.

Poorly Boy was silently admiring Buttercup, holding her on his side of the fence. All three had been silent a while (Sue apprehensively; Joan lovingly) watching Poorly Boy's rapt expression.

Joan spoke first.

"I heard you having a bad time earlier, so I thought I'd distract Poorly Boy, give you a break."

"Thanks, Joan," said Sue, feeling about as grateful as if she'd had the wrong tooth extracted, but managing not to show it.

She knew what was coming, and was irritated that Joan could nicely set them both up for it. Slowly, theatrically, as if giving over to safe hands the child of his own womb as the ship sank and he was about to drown, Buttercup was placed in the uncertain hands of his mother by her crafty son. Buttercup resplendent in apron and gold earrings and with huge eyelashes over the dumbest-looking eyes ever, smiled daftly at them from the fence top again.

'This is it,' thought Sue as Poorly Boy started his attack.

"I'm pleased Buttercup is going to have new church feet. I just wish Mr Crumble Bee could have seen the cow he should have married if you'd let him – seen her for a few minutes, that's all, before Buttercup, who would have made a beautiful Mrs Crumble Bee Cow, leaves him for ever. I'm sad she'd rather have new feet instead of being a mummy, as a mummy needs a good bee to be daddy with." He paused for a fresh breath and inspiration. "Maybe if they were together for a few minutes they'd fall in love and Crumble Cow wouldn't want the church feet any more as much as she wanted Crumble Bee." The best bit – or 'decisive punch' if you were called Sue – came last. "They could have been just like you and Mr Joan when he was alive: always together."

Sue's angry eyes glared upon her son and missed the tears in Joan's eyes.

"Buttercup is NOT going to the shed, and, what's more, you and Nelly can go and tell the purple thing he's lucky to be allowed to LIVE in the shed let alone have a wife!" Sue unpegged Nelly and gave Poorly Boy a shove in the direction of the shed. "Here, the two of you, clear off!" she added uncharitably.

"No, wait," came Joan's tiny voice. "Here Poorly Boy – just for a couple of minutes now. And don't you go getting Buttercup or Mrs Cow Crumble – whatever – dirty. I've got to be leaving soon for the fête."

"Joan!" remonstrated Sue. "You'll regret this – you know what he is!"

"I isn't anything, Mummy," said Poorly Boy, downcast, in a hurt tone which belied the sparkle in his eyes. "And Mr Crumble Bee is not a thing. He's an eminent toy surgeon and famous all over the yard for his good work saving poorly toys and even their church feet. He might even do Crumble Cow's feet for her right now; then she could stay with him all afternoon and not have to go back to church."

"Not long, I said!" laughed Joan, calling as he ran round the rear of the house towards his beloved Garden Shed Infirmary.

Mr Crumble Bee was chilling out. Uncle Peter had told Poorly Boy that when the surgeon sat on the onion pile in the corner after operations he was relaxing, chilling out. He'd been so chilling all morning, waiting for Poorly Boy to come and play with him – or better still, bring him a few patients to cut up.

Nelly burst in as the half-open door that never closed properly let the hand holding her through. There was just half an arm and Nelly visible; the rest of Poorly Boy remained hidden the door.

"We've got someone to see you, Purple Head," she said in her affectionately insulting way.

Crumble Bee, in his slow, stately drawl asked who that might be.

Little Sheeps had been rummaging around looking for nails, of which he had a fine collection as he was usually to be found somewhere about on the shed floor when not occupied as a nurse or general sheep's dogsbody, doing odd jobs for the hospital.

"It's probably your long-lost mum, Crumble Bee, come to take you to explain to your dad where you've been all this time. You once told me Mr Bumble Purple had a real temper," said Little Sheeps.

"Oh, shut up!" snapped Nelly. "Leave Crumble Bee alone and stop pulling his leg."

"All of them?" enquired Little Sheeps. "Anyway, why are you so nice to him suddenly?" he rounded on Nelly.

Nelly didn't answer, simply remarking that there wasn't much time.

Poorly Boy stepped fully inside now, with Crumble Cow held prominently in front of him.

"This is your next wife, Crumble Bee," he proclaimed grandly. "Isn't she nice?"

Crumble Bee stared at her from the onions.

"She's a cow," he drawled, more matter-of-fact than astonished.

"You didn't really expect a bee, did you?" sneered Little Sheeps. "From my experience," he continued sagely, "cows and bees do not make good marriages. It's against nature."

"No it isn't!" snapped Poorly Boy.

"What about the children? Think of them." Little Sheeps said with great feeling.

"If you can have cowboys, there's no reason why you can't have cow-bees," Poorly Boy pointed out impatiently.

During all of this, Nelly had remained silent, watching Crumble Bee and Crumble Cow watching one another.

"Are you two in love yet?" asked Poorly Boy, getting more impatient still. "Times not got all day."

No reply.

He pressed on.

"Do you want to marry each other?"

Nelly spoke for them

"No, they don't want to be married. She thinks he's ugly."

"How do you know?" Little Sheeps asked in awe.

"Because she and I are women and we understand these things. She just told me she doesn't like him."

"We didn't hear her," Poorly Boy and the sheep said together.

"We ladies have a silent language non-ladies can't hear."

"Well," replied Little Sheeps, "if that's so, Crumble Bee is telling me right now she's the most horrible cow he's ever seen – and you can't hear him as you're a woman."

Poorly Boy stepped between the overheating soft toys, both shaping up for a fight and on the verge of punching each other.

"You're going to punch each other if I don't break you up," he giggled.

"You keep out," Nelly flared at him. "You're as sheep-headed and unfeeling as he is," came the accusation.

Poorly Boy just smiled and shrugged his shoulders. The irony of the situation wasn't lost on him, however – what with Crumble Cow/Buttercup and Crumble Bee anything but lovingly looking into each other's eyes, and Nelly and Little Sheeps about to wrestle on the floor of the Garden Shed Infirmary. A fine day's work, all in all, for a place of peace and healing!

The world of Poorly Boy was a place of child magic and the quick shifts of scene imagination demands of its youngest spell-makers, who are quite grown-up when alone, and surprisingly childlike in adult company.

A short time later Joan and Sue watched Poorly Boy and Nelly skip merrily off once more towards the Garden Shed Infirmary.

"He's growing up," Joan observed, wistfully, almost sadly. "He did that with so little fuss and quite genuinely."

"No, he didn't," Sue said firmly, cynically. "He wants you to think he's being a good boy, returning Buttercup without fuss. That way he thinks you might give her to him."

"Oh, don't be cynical," the old lady reproached her. "He doesn't want me to be late for the fête, that's why. He's beginning to develop consideration for others."

Sue's eyes narrowed and said more than she did. She was puzzled why there hadn't been a scene – why Poorly Boy had thanked Joan so nicely for lending Buttercup to him, and then wished Joan and the toy cow all the best with the new feet!

"You're the most stupid sheep I've ever nursed."

Nelly was finishing bandaging Little Sheeps' right front paw with Poorly Boy's dirty handkerchief.

"I'm the only sheep you've ever nursed," he replied drily.

"Shut up, you – you ignormous! Nelly screamed at Little Sheeps.

"That's not quite the right word," offered Poorly Boy, trying to be helpful. "Uncle Peter uses big words, and – let's see – there's one a lot like you used, but not what you used."

"It'll do!" snapped Nelly, who really was in a bad mood. "We get back here after getting rid of that awful cow, and what do we find, hm? You've been insulting Mr Crumble Bee a short while before – poking nasty fun at him – and now you are begging him to take a nail out of your silly foot. You haven't even brains to gather nails without treading on one, and you've the nerve to call Mr Crumble Bee thick! If I was him, I'd tell you to clear off and get Baby Kenneth to pull it out." She was thoroughly enjoying herself.

Poorly Boy having listened intently, caught Little Sheeps' eye. The sheep looked glum, but he wasn't beaten. He whispered something to Poorly Boy, who'd bent down when he'd seen that Little Sheeps wished to say something in private.

Nelly was incensed and angrily enquired what was going on.

"He says you're only being nice to Crumble Bee because you're pleased – even thankful – he didn't get married. That way you still think you stand a chance of one day becoming Mrs Nelly Bee."

Nelly – already dyed naturally pink at the factory of her birth – went livid red, a beautiful shade of deeply embarrassed pillar box.

"I never!" she wailed.

"Go on!" taunted Poorly Boy. "As Uncle Peter says sometimes, you fancy him, don't you?"

Poor Nelly was in tears.

"Oh, you naughty boy, Poorly Boy! I'm going to tell your mum of you," she sobbed.

But Little Sheeps and Poorly Boy were too busy falling about laughing to be concerned or even hear her threat. While Nelly continued sobbing, Poorly Boy and Little Sheeps continued rolling around until both, tired and exhausted from all this fun at the poor little pink elephant's expence, lay together in a smug heap, propped up against the leg of the workbench-cum-operating table. Poorly Boy wiped the tears of laughter from his face with the dirty handkerchief before tying it back round Little Sheeps' foot. The bleeding, of course, had long since stopped.

And poor Nelly? She left this uncaring and unfeeling twosome to it, covered in straw and dirt on the floor; when accepting Mr Cromble Bee's kind invitation, she turned her back upon her horrid tormentors, to go and join him, chilling out amongst the onions.

Yes, Poorly Boy

Baby Kenneth put the phone down. He'd been calling Poorly Boy. Poorly Boy picked it off the floor, where the young rabbit dropped it, and placed it in the toy's stand.

Poorly Boy looked serious. The atmosphere was taut.

"What we need is another doctor. I'm worried about Mr Crumble Bee having too much work to do. He's going to overheat the broken dangly on his head if he's not careful." Crumble Bee's left antenna had always been rather bent.

Poorly Boy looked down at Baby Kenneth to see if he was listening. The youngster was now two and a half and beginning to talk well, though, somewhat irritatingly, always about himself.

"When I phoned just now to tell you Crumble Bee had been nasty to me again, I hoped you would get me an appointment to see another doctor," moaned Baby Kenneth, tearful, as he'd been a moment earlier when speaking on the phone to Poorly Boy.

"That's only because you're always asking him to make your poorlies better, and he can't find anything wrong with you," said Poorly Boy.

True enough, the little rabbit was going through a rather hypochondriacal stage. He looked miserable.

"You are what Mum calls a hydrocomical," offered Poorly Boy in his best profound voice.

This didn't do much to help, and Baby Kenneth promptly panicked:

"Oh will I die of it, Poorly Boy? Please tell me I won't get tummy ache with what you've just said I've got!"

Poorly Boy spent a few minutes cuddling the tearful rabbit, reassuring him that hydrocomical wasn't serious, only annoying.

Nelly was worried too. As Mr Crumble Bee's main (and only) nurse, she took a particular interest in her employer's well-being. Also, she liked him, though she'd never tell him so to his fuzzy face.

"He's too many soft-toy patients, and dead worms and things that you, Poorly Boy, want to bring back to life. That's what's the matter. Up all hours, he is, caring, operating, telling squashed ladybirds to get up and go home, they're better, as well as telling toys what they've got – or haven't got if it's Baby Kenneth. All of it by himself and me!" she said ungrammatically.

"Funny, I've been thinking that too. He needs somebody else to help him, especially with the worms. We need to get another doctor," said Poorly Boy, for once – and purely coincidentally, but almost as if he'd planned it this way – actually in agreement with Nurse Kelly.

Everyone knows the best place to find good doctors is at the local weekend market. Poorly Boy got Ben to get one there with him the very next day. It was just a block away, so they walked. On the way home they ran into Joan from next door, who gave Poorly Boy something towards the cost of treatment.

"I know what these vet's bills are," she said. "If Baby Kenneth is as expensive as my cats, you'll need twenty pence for sure."

Poorly Boy took it, thanking her, but he knew his father would pay all the bills; this would buy sweets for Baby Kenneth afterwards.

"Why is it old second-hand toys make the best doctors?" Ben was curious to know.

"Because they're older, Dad. They've had more diseases, and because they're still around they must have made themselves better," said Poorly Boy so seriously wide-eyed that it just had to be true.

Ben, bowing to such wisdom, nodded slowly.

"I see. They're more experienced, you mean."

"No, older, Dad," corrected Poorly Boy.

"What sort of doctor are we looking for?"

It was a cold winter Saturday afternoon. Ben clutched Poorly Boy's hand tightly in the crowd.

"A donkey, Dad," replied Poorly Boy firmly.

His eyes shone up at his father as they stood and surveyed the stalls in the open marketplace.

Ben was about to ask why, but he thought better of it. He'd been this way of 'asking whys' before with his son and had learnt his lesson. He was still kicking himself for that most recent why. 'What's' were OK with Poorly Boy; 'why's' took too long. He solemnly and silently nodded again – as if in profound acknowledgement of the wisdom in this 'doctor donkey' idea.

Half an hour and many stalls later, donkeys seemed in short supply, there were lots of teddies, and more exotic things like soft nylon snails. Ears and feet poked from furry shells on the most unlikely of stalls. Many of the toys were too old and battered to be of any interest to any child but Poorly Boy – who would have had them all. Many were piled ignominiously on top of one another in baskets and boxes; more and more stalls these days sell soft toys for mere pence for charitable purposes.

The light failed early, and they found themselves by the stalls near the perimeter fence.

"Come on son, – let's go home. We can go to the garden centre tomorrow and see if they've any doctors." Ben yawned, ready for his tea.

Poorly Boy was intently watching a child in a pushchair being steadily wheeled round by her mother.

"That little girl is very poorly, Dad." He and Ben had not stopped holding hands all afternoon. Ben had been afraid to let go in the crowds, which were now dwindling towards teatime. Poorly Boy tugged gently. "Let's go and see the little girl first."

Tiny was very poorly indeed, her mother told them.

Ben was not in the least embarrassed by Poorly Boy introducing the both of them with:

"I'm Poorly Boy and this is my dad. Can we help you with your poorly little girl?"

It was as if Tiny's mother was waiting for someone to open her heart to – as if, thought Ben as fleetingly as such a silly idea deserved, she was walking round the market expecting to meet Poorly Boy.

The girl was slightly younger than Poorly Boy, but she seemed much younger. She looked so frail, even beside him – and there was very little of him in physical stature. She had a serious blood disorder. As Poorly Boy made her soft toy dance gentle steps around her wrapped knees and the arms of the pushchair, the girl followed with her wide blue eyes. She seemed too weak to move a limb. Tanya – whom the name Tiny suited best – continued to follow her little playmate's delicate and cheerful games as Mrs Flint listened to Ben's explanation of his own son's illness. Her eyes were too moist, Ben noted.

Tiny's toy, Granny Gip, was a curious hedgehog. She was ancient in her bonnet and faded dress. According to Mrs Flint, the old grandmother hedgehog with the severe and stern expression had been the toy of her own mother before her. Tiny had fallen in love with it as a baby. Poorly Boy, who loved all soft toys – the vulnerable and worn most of all – told Tiny that Granny Gip was beautiful and she reminded him of his own Nelly.

"My Nelly's an elephant, but she's a bit fat too and they've got the same nice eyes."

"Could be they're related," chuckled Ben.

"Look, Tiny – see how Granny dances from one chair arm to the other? She's all excited to meet Dad and me."

The little girl continued to gaze at him, though she said nothing. Granny Gip rolled out of Poorly Boy's hand and took it upon herself to continue rolling her ball-like way over the pavement towards a stall on which they'd previously seen and examined a few toys but failed to observe any soft ones.

"Look! Pretty toys!" Tiny spoke for the first time.

They followed her frail gesture towards the stall.

Poorly boy picked up Granny Gip and stood before the stall, looking first at it, then back at Tiny. Poorly Boy pointed from one toy to the other, waiting for Tiny to stop him. She squealed as his finger found what Ben said was an elk, but which Poorly Boy knew was a donkey called Dr Donkle just as soon as he bent, lifted the corner of a foam inner cushion, and saw the donkey with the horns.

"Mum," called Poorly boy, "come and see Tiny. Her blood's gone wrong."

Sue made her way over to them, a radiantly embarrassed smile doubling as a plea for enlightenment as it fixed on Ben.

It wasn't a council of war, it was just going that way in that most unlikely place for war councils; the Garden Shed Infirmary. It had started out as a hushed-tone conference out of Baby Kenneth's big earshot as to who would go with him and Poorly Boy to the appointment. Also, with Mr Crumble Bee chilling out on the onions as usual after a hard morning's tending to the sick, Nelly was insisting everyone speak 'lowly', as she put it.

"You can't speak low enough when speaking of Crumble Bee," drawled Little Sheeps – rather too loudly for Nelly.

"Hush it. Hush it. *Hush it!*" She was yelling, observed Little Sheeps, by the time she'd reached the third of these.

Crumble Bee started to slide slowly down the onions.

"Doesn't that hurt, Crumble Bee," asked Little Sheeps with as much concern as his wide toothy grin managed when he had stifled his laughter.

Nelly pulled his ear and tenderly placed onions as a barrier at all eleven and a half legs of her employer as he arrived at the base of the pile and was about to fall off the bench.

Mr Crumble Bee continued to snore on regardless.

"Stop messing about, you two, and stop trying to get out of it. One of you's got to come, and that's it," said Poorly Boy decisively.

Nelly and Little Sheeps – together in unity for once – hugged each other in fits of laughter.

"We work for Mr Crumble Bee," said Little Sheeps regally, not you Poorly Boy."

Poorly Boy had just collected himself together from the shock of this, his soft toys' rebellion against his authority, and he was about to go for Little Sheeps especially, for such a blatant show of hypocrisy.

"You're a nasty, smelly sheep, you are," he said. "Uncle Peter would call you two-faced, and I'll tell you for why." But he didn't. That was as far as he got.

By this time, things had got loud enough for ants' let alone rabbit's ears.

"Oh, Nelly, please come with me to see Dr Thiny. I don't know him and you can stop him cutting me up for pies and mouse food," wailed Baby Kenneth – typically rabbits at very last moments decide against things they previously wanted to do. He always started impassioned sentences with 'oh', rabbits at his tender-age being melodramatic creatures. He found he got his own way more often when he began with a winsome 'oh'.

"Pies and mouse food!" blurted out Little Sheeps, almost falling off the bench edge as Nelly bashed him on the head with her trunk, telling him to keep the noise down.

If Crumble Bee had woken suddenly, he'd have ridden on his onion barrier as it turned into ball bearings and conveyed him over the edge and across the floor.

Nelly sighed.

"I'll come, then, silly rabbit. Stop crying."

Baby Kenneth thanked his lucky *ohs* and smiled angelically.

"Tell Little Sheeps to take care of Crumble Bee, will you, Nelly?" said Poorly Boy coyly. "He won't listen to me." He managed a shot at Little Sheeps, however, with, "But it is Nelly that Baby Kenneth wants to go with us and not you."

It was Nelly's day and she was enjoying it. The hapless Little Sheeps was left with instructions to make sure Crumble Bee didn't launch himself into dark shed corners.

"How?" was his forlorn enquiry.

"You'll find a way," Nelly assured him as she stood by the door in Poorly Boy's hand. "You've just said, if not in so many words, that his brain power was *low*, unlike yours; stopping him ending up on the floor shouldn't be too difficult for such a clever sheep."

Poorly Boy grinned and nodded his head slightly down and to the right – a kind of 'that's telling you' nod at Little Sheeps.

In the car, Nelly continued to be commanding and authoritative, telling Poorly Boy and Ben, while driving to Tiny's home, that if she didn't consider Dr Donkle's nurse, whoever she was, a good one, she wouldn't let her touch Baby Kenneth. Baby Kenneth lapped this up as if he were a cat, not a rabbit.

"All we want to do is get the new doctor to tell us how to make you better, isn't it, Dad?" Poorly Boy looked at Ben for help as they approached the house on the outskirts of town.

"Er, that's all. Dr Donkle was so good with Tiny – as she seemed to know he would be as soon as she picked, er, found him – that Pee Bee decided to leave him with her. Er, rather her with him, I mean. No, that's it – silly me! It was Dr Donkle who suggested he stay with her."

Fortunately, the driving didn't suffer during this flannelling. Ben felt Poorly Boy's disappointment. It hurt him that maybe he wasn't rising to meet the occasion quite as the lad expected.

"Granny Gip, of course, is a fully trained nurse – isn't she, Pee Bee? – as you'd expect."

'That's more like it.' Ben thought, on a wave of confident inspiration meant to please his son.

Poorly Boy looked surprised.

"I don't remember that, Dad."

"Yes you do." Ben exasperatedly prodded Poorly Boy.

"Can't possibly have forgotten already, Pee Bee."

Poorly Boy, slow for once, caught on.

"Yes, Dad. Fancy me forgetting that! Said he could tell Baby Kenneth if he was poorly or not; and, like that Mr Crumble Bee, he was sure there was nothing wrong."

Baby Kenneth started to cry once more, not wanting to be that well.

Mrs Flint couldn't believe the change in her daughter since meeting Poorly Boy the day before. He'd given her little girl eyes again – big sparkly ones, not just two dark sunken sockets that rarely came out to play. And Granny Gip – Mrs Flint had never seen her so animated and alive, even after Poorly Boy went home.

As a sick child, Tiny had little energy for that special place where children go to talk to their toys. Poorly Boy, ill that he was himself, had a way with soft toys that soft toys loved. He made the shy things want to talk on their own terms and enter the world of humans.

Tanya's mother was with her daughter, watching, waiting for Poorly Boy and Ben to arrive. Granny Gip was busy, bossing Tiny, telling her to stop slopping her drink down her front, and fussily dabbing her dress with a tissue while going on about what a naughty and unruly girl Tiny was. Usually – before Poorly Boy – all Granny Gip did was sit still and silently by, watching. For the first time since Tiny's birth, her mother was the watcher and Tiny was doing – and doing as Granny Gip told her.

That moment in the market, when Poorly Boy's own mother had come up to them and the two women instantly shared the bond of having sick children, began a sort of healing for Mrs Flint herself – especially since there was no one really close to her since her marriage break-up.

The doorbell rang and Baby Kenneth, still crying and being told for the umpteenth time there was nothing to fear, was pushed reluctantly into Poorly Boy's hand by Nelly and him through the door followed by Ben.

"He thinks Dr Donkle will kick him, Mrs Flint, if he's not poorly enough to have medicine. Little Sheeps told him donkey doctors kick you if you waste their time. Anyway, he doesn't want to have no poorlies at all, 'cos then he'd have nothing to be hydrocomical about," explained Poorly Boy brightly.

"Little Sheeps has a dark sense of humour," added Ben by way of clarification.

Nelly had no time for this. She hurried the screaming rabbit, kicking and fighting most unpoorly-like, in to see Dr Donkle, who was just beginning to tend to Tiny in the living room he was using as his surgery. Granny Gip grabbed Baby Kenneth and stuck him in front of the doctor on Tiny's knee.

Nelly had allowed Dr Donkle's nurse to take over because she immediately recognised Granny Gip as her own long-lost great-greatest grandmother too.

Poorly Boy was letting everyone know what was happening with a running commentary.

"But she's a hedgehog and –"

Poorly Boy cut the sentence off.

"That don't matter, Dad. Nelly's going on, saying she's no ladies to talk to apart from Mum, if she's in the right mood, and that all of us boss her."

"Seems to me she bosses you lot far more," Ben observed.

"Don't Dad," said Poorly Boy with much concern. "If she hears you she'll get on to us."

Dad passed over these incongruities and went on: "Your Dr Donkle's a bit rough with his examination technique. Why is he holding Baby Kenneth upside down?"

"Because he has one of his poorlies there, Dad, and Mr Crumble Bee said he couldn't find his brain, so he thought it might be that. Dr Donkle's thinking if Baby Kenneth's brain falls out shaking him, he can clean it and put it back. If not, then it can't be that that's aching."

Tiny, meanwhile, thought this splendid fun. Those eyes Poorly Boy had made her a gift of shone from sockets that had been without eyes for a long time. It was as if they were lit from behind by a torch which Poorly Boy had put there.

'*Maybe he had.*' thought Ben.

After much shaking, diagnosing, laughing and healing, and with Nelly and her great-greatest grandmother hugging and catching up on the lost years, Dr Donkle was ready to give his verdict and treatment. Poorly Boy spoke for him, as important doctors always have others to speak for them.

"Baby Kenneth's got a sore bottom because he won't wipe it properly. It's spread all over his paws."

Ben wondered what had, but didn't ask.

"His head aches because he won't eat his greens."

"How's he going to treat it?" asked Ben, feeling part of a double act.

"He's got to wipe his bottom better – and take lots of Donkle rides round at Tiny's. So we have to keep coming here unless Baby Kenneth's too poorly, and then him and Granny Gip and Tiny have to come to us," replied Poorly Boy, grinning mischievously.

In fact, the Donkle rides became a major part of the cures. They were his cures, actually, and Baby Kenneth spent the time until going home, happily being treated, seated on the elk's back (for in truth he was an elk, just as Ben had said he was).

As the young rabbit's condition improved, so did Tiny's. She was receiving similar treatment, slightly modified. She wasn't to get on the Doctor's back, but to let the small brown soft toy bounce its rides up and down in her hand whenever she felt the need. Granny Gip always told her how good this special treatment was, and that she would soon be well – just like Baby Kenneth.

Ben, who felt from the beginning of this saga like the straight-man part of the act, thought he might well end it in this vein:

"How did you know you were going to meet a little girl at the market who also wanted a donkey toy, Pee Bee?" he asked as they drove home.

They had been listening to Nelly going on about Granny Gip while Baby Kenneth serenaded them with a rabbit song.

"I didn't, Dad. It's just that I like donkeys, and when she picked one we'd missed, with horns on like a big deer, I thought, 'She's a very poorly person and she could do with him to go live with her'."

"Is that why you paid for her with your own twenty pence?"

"Yes, Dad," said Poorly Boy.

"Yes, Poorly Boy," said Ben.

Ben rarely said 'Poorly Boy', and Poorly Boy was surprised.

"I don't like you saying that, Dad. I like you to say Pee Bee. The way you say Poorly Boy sounds all serious."

"What sort of sweeties does Baby Kenneth want?" said Ben.

Baby Kenneth's Weekend

Baby Kenneth was not a good swimmer. Poorly Boy had for hours been trying to teach him in the orange plastic swimming pool, the one Sue was about to take over to wash up in. An argument developed.

"It'll have to wait until I've done the lunchtime things; then I might – if you're a good boy – dry Baby Kenneth's bathing costume."

This, of course, was Baby Kenneth's everything costume, as Poorly Boy had merely dunked the poor thing so that right now it was one unpleasantly soft, soggy toy.

Poorly Boy, trailing the miserable spectacle, followed his mother inside, grumbling and awkward as only a five-year-old with no intention of being good can be.

"If he catches cold and dies, it's your fault." scolded Poorly Boy.

"Take him to your precious Mr Crumble Bee. He'll sort him out if he's dying."

"Drying – he wants drying," replied Poorly Boy exasperatedly, as if he were talking to an idiot. "All right" he added resolutely a short pause later. "I will go and see Crumble Bee. He's helpful and loving and kind – and he wouldn't put a few dirty cups and plates before a poorly, poorly baby rabbit!" he snapped.

"He's not poorly – he's wet," countered Sue drily.

Poorly Boy flounced off to the Garden Shed Infirmary, dragging Baby Kenneth behind him.

"Dad, where can we keep Joey? He can't stop in the shed, because Crumble Bee's frightened of him."

Ben was dozing in the lounge, home after another long haul in his lorry. His son's gentle tones brought him contentedly awake, one eye open. It was good to be home with the little fellow and the family.

"Pee Bee, what's on your shoulder?" Ben's eyes were both very much open, his voice going from low-high to soft-low in shocked, slow seconds.

"It's Joey, Dad. He came and nested on me – flew through the shed doors. Isn't he nice, Dad?"

Ben was not able to answer this.

"Me and Crumble Bee was drying Baby Kenneth out from swimming and I was helping when Joey came in. He'd been watching us swimming and thought Baby Kenneth would like to be his friend. They're both the same age and colour – see, Dad. He's nesting, so he's pulling my hair out. Let's go buy him a cage and let him live here, where he can be close to Kenneth. He wants to be the boss of him as they're the same size."

Ben was slowly rising, gingerly approaching the little blue budgie busily nest-making on Poorly Boy's shoulder. There came a scream from the kitchen end of the lounge behind them. Joey relocated his nest site promptly up to the rod fixing the room light to the ceiling.

"You've scared him now," said Poorly Boy angrily. "He's gone away from his best nest because of you, Mum. That was daft screaming. How's he going to live with you if you scare him like that?"

"Now you know you'll only worry about putting weight on if you have too much." Ben in quiet desperation was trying to restore some semblance of normality. He placed the teacup on the kitchen table. Sue's hand was too unsteady to take it from him. Usually she took no sugar; if stressed she took one. Today she'd nodded on 'three' as he counted, "One? Two? Three?"

Ben seated himself at the other end of the table, facing her. Neither spoke. Poorly Boy could be heard falling around the room next door. Occasionally there came an ominous crashing.

"His heart? What about his heart?" intoned Sue mournfully.

Ben wondered, but didn't ask, if she meant the budgie's or Poorly Boy's. 'Knowing my son's sense of adventure and enthusiasm, probably the budgie's heart will feel the strain first,' Ben thought but didn't say. He knew his son better then anyone – even though his job dictated long days away. He had a kind of instinct concerning Pee Bee's health. No red lights were on at the moment – indeed, it seemed as though his heart could cope very well with fuss and excitement, as though the boy's strong spirit looked after the ailing heart. He'd seen his son, purple-lipped and eyes as dark as if he were wearing goggles and yet he knew – no matter how much Sue might fret at such times – that Poorly Boy would be OK. The intensity of his son's extraordinary inner life left the lad often drained physically – but elated, happy and somehow getting along and managing the potentially serious illness. Time alone would tell if Poorly Boy's spirit was enough – no matter how gloomy the medical prognosis.

Ben suddenly realised there had been no sound from the lounge for some time now. Sue, he knew long before their marriage, had a genuine phobia against 'flying things', as she put it. Even butterflies in the house terrified her. Ben was staring at the lounge door as it slowly began to open.

"Daddy, don't make a noise and come in here."

Again he found himself reticently crossing the floor.

"I thought, seeing as Baby Kenneth and Joey was friends, I'd fetch him to get Joey off the rail we hang the pictures on."

Poorly Boy was following his father around, tidying up. Nothing seemed broken – despite the crashes – but cushions, chairs and pictures had been either upended or skewwhiffed.

Poorly Boy babbled on: "So I brought him out to the Garden Shed Infirmary and sat him on the shiny table."

"The highly polished table," noted Ben ruefully.

A sodden Baby Kenneth, seated in an overflowing pond dripping carpet-wards, was still upon the said table being chirruped to and beak-punched earnestly by his new best buddy.

"God help us if Sue comes in?" Ben muttered.

"Ben," came Sue's shaky voice, "can I come in now? Have you got it yet?"

"Yes, Mum," chirruped Poorly Boy, "you can come in. Everything's great."

'Mum and Joey were having a lovely time running about the lounge,' thought Poorly Boy.

"He's awfully pleased you like him, Mum," beamed Poorly Boy, chasing after the three of them – Sue, Joey and Ben. "If you stop shouting, he might settle and talk to Kenneth again. Then we can have some tea." Poorly Boy had suddenly decided he was hungry after so much fun.

Uncle Peter was not sure. He wasn't one for pets. The idea of Baby Kenneth with him for every meal, and having to go with him everywhere in the house, was worrying. Plus sleeping on the pillow beside him! But he'd promised his nephew, and he wouldn't betray a tearful Poorly Boy. Uncle Peter hated to see the child cry, and perhaps this was the most upset he'd seen him. Ben had phoned on the previous evening, pleading with him to take the stray budgie. Sue was hysterical and had locked herself in the bathroom, threatening not to come out until Joey was gone. The five-year-old couldn't understand why his mother disliked the little blue bird so.

Ben was right now sitting nursing his son, rocking him, trying once more to explain why Joey had to go to Uncle Peter.

His small face swollen with crying, Poorly Boy jumped down. He made his way over to his uncle and looked solemnly up at him. His eyes were red-rimmed.

"Don't let Baby Kenneth snore, Uncle Peter. It's bad for his tummy to snore if he's had a big supper."

'Poorly Boy must have half heard some conversation between Ben and Sue about snoring,' thought Uncle Peter.

"Of course I won't let him snore on a full stomach, old son."

Uncle Peter made himself sound as sympathetic as possible while almost laughing despite himself.

Poorly Boy wiped his running nose on his sleeve.

"Daddy have you got Baby Kenneth's soap and toothbrush?"

Benn stood behind his son and handed the plastic supermarket bag with the soft toy's overnight things to Uncle Peter. Both the giving and the receiving was as if the bag contained lead weights. They watched Poorly Boy take the blue rabbit into the front room, where Joey's cage was. They left him alone in there whilst he placed the toy on a table piled with books so Joey could see his friend from the cage on its stand.

Sue felt like a monster. She had tried to make the boy understand her irrational fears. Tenderly, patiently she'd gone over it, answering his questions as best she could – yet still she was guilt-ridden.

"Don't cry Mummy," he'd said, tears in his big eyes, as much for her distress, she felt, as for his own. "I've seen little girls frightened of spiders and creepies, so I know that you, when a little girl, were frightened of birds and flappy things. And even when you're grown-up birds flap like they did then – so you will be just as scared."

"Ben, he's heartbroken." Sue's face was as swollen as her son's.

"But he'll get over it. He's resilient and, though he's disappointed, he understands in his own way." Ben felt wretched. His words were empty and unconvincing and he knew it.

Next day Poorly Boy helped his father in the garden. It was spring and, with Ben away so much, chores about the house and garden always awaited his attention on his return home. As a rule, Poorly Boy loved these times of pottering after his father. The ambulance/wheelbarrow with the team of soft toys on board was parked at the lawn edge while Nelly or Little Sheeps, or one of the others, sat on the path, Poorly Boy chittering to them as he 'weeded the lawn'. Ben was surprised to find today no different to other such occasions. Poorly Boy was quite his usual cheerful and happy self. It was almost as if Joey had never existed, his name being mentioned not once.

Robert

The train moved off and stopped. It wasn't the points or the possibility of a head-on collision round the bend that held it, but the hand of Fate. All on board were in Fate's hand – and they knew it.

The passengers on this train were not happy travellers. Fate's hand let go a moment and went round to the front of the train, where, being attached to Fate's arm, it placed itself palm down and drummed its fingers on the book of Fate – or rather *Fate's Annual of Captain Flat Worm* stories.

Fate's eye placed itself on a level with the train, while the other eye closed tightly to give more concentrated effort to the one seeing eye.

"If I was older, I could have an electric one of these," Fate remarked.

"Yes, and while your dad's wiring it up, he might even wire a switch for your brain when he does the on switch for the train. Or maybe just the one switch would do for both."

To this reply – no way, by the way, to speak to Fate – came another reply from the top of the carriage, a carriage's length behind the reply from the first carriage.

It replied, "No brain to wire it to."

"Are you ready?" yawned Sue, idly flicking the pages of a child's comic as she lay on the floor down lane from Fate. "Baby Kenneth's just told me he's sick of waiting for Nelly to get hurt."

Fate angrily heaved himself up on his arms and became Poorly Boy.

"He never 'cos he doesn't talk to you, only me, and he doesn't say 'hurt', only 'deaded'."

"No, he doesn't, clever! And don't say 'deaded'; it's ignorant," contradicted Sue, correcting Poorly Boy's grammar. She turned the page and got to the exciting bit where Captain Flat Worm (he of the big Fate's Annual fame from earlier) smote Wicked Ladybird with a series of the usual deft Captain

Flat Worm smites. "Any young rabbit who's of an age when he's able to take computer lessons every second Tuesday is old enough to use 'hurt' instead of the rather rabbit-ish 'deaded'."

Poorly Boy stood, clenching his tiny fists, all fuss and temper, and glared at Sue.

"He's not going computering till Uncle Peter comes, and till then he'll do as he's told – and even after then he'll do as he's told. So if he says 'deaded', then he says 'deaded'!"

Sue sighed and, pushing the comic annual aside, give in and laid her cheek flat on the carpet. Baby Kenneth was an arm's length to her right.

"OK, tell me when you want us to start our emergency drill to save Nelly and Little Sheeps from the train crashing into the tunnel."

"No, no, no!" stormed Poorly boy. "You're deliberately getting it wrong. There's not going to be a crash in it. Nelly and Little Sheeps are going to get knocked off before it, because they're on the roofs but won't go through! I airplaned all that before."

"Explained," corrected Sue airily.

"That as well," said Poorly Boy.

Poorly Boy, Sue and the two team members who were endangered species, plus baby Kenneth, were practising their 'disaster-response drill', as Sue called it. Poorly Boy called it 'crash plastering', as in plastering wounds up after crashing. They did this drill periodically, whenever Poorly Boy felt the team needed a refresher course in watching him lose his temper.

He wouldn't have seen it this way; he preferred to see it as making sure everybody knew what to do if there was an accident or disaster. Actually, though, the former description fitted better. If anyone was on the verge of disaster or accident, it was Poorly Boy – by falling over something in his rage. He really did expect a lot from the team – and Sue.

"You're far too tough with the team. You bully them."

"No, I don't at all, Mum. You've seen on telly how in those movies when bridges fall down and airplanes lose their wings all the rescuers say lots of things to each nuvers when they're busy rescuing. They talk all the way through the saving of people's lives. I want my team to be able to rescue while talking all the time as well."

Sue giggled, rolled over on her back and informed Poorly Boy that real life wasn't like the movies and the best rescuers keep their mouths shut; they just get on and do it. But of course Poorly Boy knew different. Today he was in one of those splendid 'knowing different to everyone else' moods that five-year-olds (and the rest of us) have at times.

This morning's drill had Nelly and Little Sheeps sitting astride the roof of Poorly Boy's push-along train. The tunnel, seemingly bent on cutting off their heads, was to be thwarted in its nefarious deed by a derailment involving Sue's finger just before the tunnel entrance.

"If you don't derail us safely and in comfort before we're beheaded, I'll never speak to you again," warned Nelly quietly into Poorly Boy's ear as he lay beside her, about to move the train off.

"And I promise on Nocky's knock knees I'll never make you laugh again at nasty things I say about Nelly and Crumble Bee being in love, if you kill me," threatened Little Sheeps, looking from the rear of Poorly Boy's ear.

"Don't worry, you two sillies," Poorly Boy reassured them, facing down line towards Sue.

Still on her back, unaware of this exchange, Sue bounced Baby Kenneth about in the air above her, arms stretched full length upwards, holding his paws.

"They're having a great time, aren't they?" observed Little Sheeps.

"You wait till Mum's finger gets run over and you come safely off the roof, parachuted down in my hand. Baby Kenneth'll bawl his tail sore with sitting on it, crying!"

Poorly Boy thought this remark very clever and didn't catch Little Sheeps and Nelly looking at each other with very dry looks indeed – not until he turned their way anyway.

"You do trust me, don't you!" (He'd seen something in their eyes.)

"No!" they said in rare and absolute unanimity.

Poorly Boy started to push the engine and train forward.

A fairly quiet town with reasonably decent villains and a population of ordinary troublesome folk, neither too bad nor too good, does have its moments. Uncle Peter had reported on many of these people's moments – how their lives became like the lives of their readers, with loves going wrong or events taking over. Their readers and, indeed, their reporters!

Uncle Peter had reported many such moments and seen things he'd not like his young nephew, his sister or his brother-in-law to see. But how was he going to avoid this moment? Firstly, he didn't want Poorly Boy to see what looked like a car stranded on the traffic island just now. Secondly – ah, secondly – he felt too wretched simply to walk. His heart, as they say, was heavy – too heavy for the fattest of Cupids to heave around.

The light-green gate, with the safety catch as safe as Poorly Boy wanted everyone to think it was, snicked behind him. Uncle Peter braced himself for the fiction he wasn't about to write but tell. As he approached the green gate in thought, he remembered to start limping slightly. Either his nephew or Baby Kenneth must have seen him coming (they'd be expecting him at this time on every second Tuesday anyway).

Which of them saw him first, Uncle Peter couldn't tell, but Poorly Boy's distant gleeful voice sounded from inside a second before Baby Kenneth's blue floppy ears flopped through the letterbox from inside out.

Poorly Boy's voice, much louder now, followed the ears from inside the same oblong hole in the door:

"Want a bun, Uncle Peter, wiv a teacup before we go? We were going to have a train crash but Baby Kenneth got scared Nelly would get hurt – and when Little Sheeps started to make fun of him, saying there was no use him falling in love with Nelly because she was all gooey about Crumble Bee, he ran away into the hall just about the same time saw you coming from the window, which was just after the clock said you should be here. Door's not locked. Come on."

Poorly Boy and Baby Kenneth dragged Uncle Peter through the partly opened door with a bit of a knee bump and shoulder thump, but nothing too serious to dampen Uncle Peter's spirits, momentarily uplifted at the exuberance of the welcome.

"Least somebody still loves me," he chuckled.

"Oh, 'course we do, Uncle Peter. We loves yous because yous the bestest reporter and poet the office has ever seen. In't that so, Baby Kenneth?"

The young blue rabbit's ears flapped in exuberant affirmation with such gusto that he flew out of Poorly Boy's hand right up at Uncle Peter's face and kissed him before dropping down to polish his hero's trainers.

"What adulation! What fame!" enthused Uncle Peter, despite his underlying sorrowful and morose mood. "I've a bit of a bad leg today," he continued.

"How did you do that? Do you want an appointment with Mr Crumble Bee? He's not got anyone to do for a while and he's real good at legs – remember Little Sheeps?"

Uncle Peter did remember how Crumble Bee, the talk of every dying flower in the garden, had recommended Little Sheeps be kept moving as aid to setting his broken legs after Poorly Boy had tossed him on the floor in temper.

"No, thanks," Uncle Peter declined. "It'll go when the weather turns warmer – just rheumatism from an old football injury."

"Mr Crumble Bee's great with injured footballs," said Poorly Boy persistently. "He squishes them and puts them to rest."

"I see. So they're limp, is that it?" enquired Uncle Peter.

"They don't limp, Uncle Peter," came the reply, "not in bed anyway."

Sue was smiling like someone who was looking forward to being five-year-old-less and alone with Little Sheeps for a few hours.

"What's this about injured ex-footballers? You are still going to the office with Poorly Boy, aren't you, Peter?" Her face dropped as the dark possibility he might not be going suddenly grabbed hold of it, pulling it downwards.

"Er, yes, of course – only we'll be going in my car and not parking it up here in the garage drive as we usually do. We'd better go the direct way also, so I've as little gear-changing work as possible with the poor old foot." He turned to Poorly Boy: "That'll mean we won't be going by the traffic island, I'm afraid, old son." He smiled, weakly apologetic.

"Aw, Uncle Peter, I love rounding the roundabout – but if your foot's sick I don't mind. 'Course I don't!" he said cheerfully.

"Maybe by tonight your foot will feel better and we can come home that way."

That was OK with Uncle Peter, although he didn't say so. By evening the police should have cleared what appeared at a swift, horrified glance to be a battered old Vauxhall stranded way up on the island flower beds with a teddy bear trapped in the rear door by its arm.

Uncle Peter was pleased with himself. For long enough, every second Tuesday when he and Clive (the photographer) had a day off, talking over future projects he and Poorly Boy walked the shortish distance to the office via the traffic island if it was fine. Poorly Boy loved to spend a few minutes, both ways, watching the traffic while clutching Baby Kenneth and Nelly – his usual companions on the office venture. Those hours at the newspaper headquarters spent with the office girls ('For lucky Poorly Boy and his two team members,' mused Uncle Peter) while the girls gave the blue rabbit computer lessons, and the reporter and his photographer mulled professional matters over in an adjacent room.

Poorly Boy understood fully that the poorly leg and/or foot meant they'd have to go by car today – the shortest possible way.

"Let's have a final check. Knowing you, you'll get there and find you've forgotten Baby Kenneth's dummy or something."

Sue was used to this.

Poorly Boy remembered he'd forgotten Baby Kenneth's carrot dummy, and Sue went away and reappeared with a baby-prepared one out of a child's luncheon pack of baby carrots.

"Good thing I thought to check!"

Poorly Boy jauntily shoved the dummy, blue-rabbit-nose-wards.

"Aren't I a good organoser?" he sighed as if exasperated at everyone's inefficiency.

Nelly made sure she wasn't left behind with the sardonic Little Sheeps on the railway track as she loved to be spoilt by the office girls and certainly didn't fancy a Spartan day stranded and railway-carriaged with a sarcastic woolly sheep.

Uncle Peter hobbled theatrically to the car assisted by Nurse Nelly and Poorly Boy's arm holding her around Uncle Peter's knee.

"Oh, isn't it painful?" Sue asked her younger brother flashing a glance at her ironical tone. "Shouldn't you have it X-rayed?"

"No, Mum," Poorly Boy replied on behalf of his uncle as he opened the car door for him while Nelly held Uncle Peter's knee, presumably propping him up as he leant on the roof. "Uncle doesn't want none of those because they burn you like when I put Little Sheeps too near the toaster. You said so yourself that he smelt like they'd X-rayed his ears and forgot to switch the machine off."

"Go on, you lot! Keep out of my hair for a few hours," chided Sue.

She waved them away, wondering what really was wrong with her younger brother – as if she didn't know. She'd seen that look on his face a few times, and she knew what was behind it. It wasn't a leg – unless a far more shapely one than his own. Uncle Peter was about to wipe his mental brow with his brilliant imitation of a man with either a poorly leg or poorly foot and pat his inventiveness and acting ability on the cerebral back, when he turned the corner on the short journey to the office. A huge yellow diversion sign, on account of a students' rag-week procession it wanted him to know about, was coming his way. It met him at the roadside to inform him of its decision to re-route the traffic via the roundabout. He groaned.

"What's it say, Uncle Peter?" Poorly Boy exclaimed. "Well, isn't that funny, Uncle! You'd never believe it unless Nelly and me and Baby Kenneth were here to see it with you, would you?"

Like a man deflated by many defeats who's lost his will even to be defeated, Uncle Peter followed the detour.

"Uncle Peter," came the voice, "what do the students want rags for?"

Uncle Peter motored doomily on.

"That daft man in the van just tooted us, Uncle Peter. What's he do that for? We're not in his way. Aren't some people incondurate?"

"Indeed they are – and there are some daft road signs," replied Uncle Peter enigmatically, closing moment by moment on the inevitable.

"Aw, Uncle Peter, look at that crashed car on the flower bed with those gnomes and dwarves all round it. Isn't that a sight!"

Uncle Peter almost lost control of nerves and car. Fortunately the roundabout wasn't a busy one, and he drove on at a more steady pace than earlier. The crashed car appeared to be decidedly more bent by wear and age than by collision, with its attendant dwarves, gnomes and elves scattered around the island. And was that or was that not Clive who buys me a drink at the office, waving us to pull over and do something about that poor, poor teddy trapped by his arm in the car's back door?"

So many questions for one day? Uncle Peter didn't care any more. He pulled in behind a parked police car. One officer was on the radio; one was directing proceedings amongst the gnomes and Robin on the traffic island. Uncle Peter didn't in truth feel at all well. It was his head, not his leg, that hurt. He sat wondering what to do as Robin Clive came towards him. Nelly and Baby Kenneth were gazing at the sight through the window with a silent, open-mouthed Poorly Boy. Silence and the open mouth were usually a bad combination with Poorly Boy, presaging the fruition of some master plan or other.

"Morning, Pete. Morning, Nelly, Baby Kenneth and you, my lad." Clive, brightly upbeat, rested an elbow and forearm on the open-car-window ledge.

"Coleman phoned me to get down here sharpish and get photos. Suppose he got you to come too?"

It wasn't turning out the way Uncle Peter had planned it at all.

"Nelly finks we ought to go and rescue that teddy bear, Uncle Peter."

Uncle Peter shut his eyes tightly and squeezed the gear lever more tightly.

"What a great idea, Poorly Boy!" said Clive enthusiastically. "The poor thing does look miserable and woebegone."

"If we get him out alive, we can take him back to the children he belongs to – once Mr Crumble Bee has operated on him and made him better," suggested Poorly Boy.

Clive opened the passenger door and helped Poorly Boy out from the rear seat.

"You stay here, Peter. You don't look at all well. We'll handle this. I'll get clicking."

Poorly Boy, Clive, Nelly and Baby Kenneth trotted over the road to the traffic island. Uncle Peter watched, making no effort to follow. This was not like him – the exuberant, witty one, the rightful aider and abetter in Poorly Boy's escapades.

The passenger door opened and Geraldine slipped in, her hand alighting on his knee.

"Peter, I'm so sorry. Last night – forgive me."

Geraldine, newest member from out of town on the reporting staff; Geraldine of the long golden hair; Geraldine of Uncle Peter's lost heart walked across beside a beaming Uncle Peter to the operation scene.

"Geraldine's here to report after Coleman phoned her. I'm at a loose end, I guess, so can I help?" Uncle Peter asked sheepishly.

"Shush, Uncle. Clive's given teddy some Vick's to put him to sleep, and I'm telling Clive how to get the trapped arm free."

Uncle Peter felt and looked woebegone. God, he was jealous. Geraldine knew, and she blinked a long, slow green-eyed blink and squeezed his hand reassuringly. Uncle Peter felt at once quite content to stay out of this one.

"One of the students with a big card hung round his neck pranced up to them. Robert bowed low and courtly in his medieval-cum-gnome costume. Without a word he bent forward, kissed Poorly Boy on the head, knelt before the trapped teddy, opened the door with a key, and let the teddy free. Poorly Boy, amazed, enthralled and hypnotised all at once, stood and felt his arms being gently folded about the teddy as Robert laid him against Poorly Boy's chest. Nelly was still clutched in one hand and Baby Kenneth in the other, forming a cross. Robert stepped back as Poorly Boy knelt again. Robert bowed deeply from the waist with a fine sweep of his right arm, brushing the grass before him at his feet in front of Poorly Boy with his fingers and the feather in his hat. Then Robert unlocked the front door, wound the window down, smiled broadly, turned the ignition and, amidst clouds of bang and smoke of black, drove the car forwards. As it chugged, the smoke exhumed the strategically placed wooden planks, hitherto, unnoticed, protecting the flower bed from harm across the grass divide where one bed ended and another began. Two tyres were on the close-cropped remainder of the island. The scene was instantly returned to its virgin condition, and everyone drifted college-, home-, office- or town-wards.

Baby Kenneth's computer lesson was shared that Tuesday with his new friend, a teddy called Robert, with whom Geraldine had fallen in love. Baby Kenneth suggested she take him home to live with her and, seeing as he was such an expert with computers, he continued (for the time at least) to teach Baby Kenneth every second Tuesday.

Interstellar Tomcats

Sometimes, when Pat returned to square up the untidy bedroom in Poorly Boy's head, it so happened that Nelly couldn't sleep either.

This particular night the little pink elephant was cuddling Baby Kenneth so tight that he couldn't sleep either. Poorly Boy, because Nelly seemed so unhappy and tearful, knew he'd have to do something to take their minds off the bossy little girl with the tropical-fish-tank-rimmed eyes who'd been Nelly's mother and Poorly Boy's during his stay in hospital.

"But Pat will come to us one day – I know it, Nelly. She's taking her time, that's all. She wants to be sure she's not missed any poorly toys in heaven before she brings them to us for making better."

Nurse Nelly was silent. Her tiny black eyes looked up at him sadly – and there was a hint of not believing in them? Poorly Boy had to move fast.

"I'll tell you a story to get us to sleep. Stop squeezing the stuffing out of Baby Kenneth and listen."

Poorly Boy's brow bent wavy as his lids pulled down to rummage desperately deep inside the untidy bedroom where Pat was busy, to see if they could spot a story. A cat made a noise outside. Poorly Boy's eyes, searching the inside room's every corner, saw Pat throw aside the curtains in a huff to let more starlight into the cluttered muddle of her adopted son's bedroom in the head. His mouth dropped open a little as Uncle Peter, looking in through the window, pointed and silently mouthed the title of the book Poorly Boy and his uncle often read together: *Interstellar Observations*. It was a big name for pages full of lovely-sounding words, which the amateur astronomer tried to explain to his nephew.

"It's about interstellar tomcats!" exclaimed Poorly Boy after what seemed to him a long silence, but which was in fact, only long enough for a cat howl to collide with a night sky and Uncle Peter to drop in. "Interstellar toms," he repeated slowly, savouring the syllable sounds of it and the kind of drawn out miaow they made.

There was one slight pause further, to get Nelly, Kenneth and the Christmas Fairy comfy together on his pillow whilst he arranged himself cross-legged and smothered round with his warm hyena-flowered bed rug, as he called it, but he still wasn't ready. Surely any onlooker sleeplessly, lazily gazing for sheep in the black-that-isn't of a summer night would have seen Poorly Boy floating with his hyena (or hyacinth) rug, off to the deep-space prowling grounds of interplanetary felines.

But the Christmas Fairy wanted a wee. He'd begged her from Sue during his first Christmas out of hospital, figuring she was the nearest to an angel he'd get until Pat came back with other angels carrying those poorly toys for his care. Whenever Pat had a mind to tidy his room, the Christmas Fairy came to stay the night with Poorly Boy, out of the way and out of the cupboard.

"Right, is everybody happy now?" said Poorly Boy crossly. "Any more playing about and bathrooms, and I won't tell the story."

Baby Kenneth started to cry at having to wait so long, and his beloved Poorly Boy was forced to get angry and threaten no story. A few more minutes were lost whilst the baby rabbit was consoled and reassured that the story would continue as soon as he stopped sobbing. Such interruptions, though undoubtedly frustrating for the storyteller, did afford time to make the story up.

When, however, he announced it wasn't so much a story as a true description of how these real space cats really live, that was it. He'd overreached himself before he'd got truly started. Baby Kenneth started to cry once more. Poorly Boy, realising he'd maybe gone a bit too far with all his real stuff, hastily assured Baby Kenneth that, though not a true story as such, it would be very exciting nonetheless.

He caught a quick and rather panicky glimpse of Pat holding up a painting Crumble Bee did of a striped cat he'd seen on the TV. She put her head right, then left, then wrinkled her face as if the cat smelt, and threw it out of the door where all the other rubbish from the inner room was going.

"Galactic cat flaps – or intergalactic cat flaps, which is their proper name – let the interstellar tomcats in and out of each galaxy, which is a big, big place where stars live. These flaps with hinges to go both ways are what scientists call black holes, only there's green and mauve ones too. If they were all black, the toms wouldn't find them – or those with bad eyes wouldn't, as space is black too, you see. It's just no one down here has seen the green and mauve ones yet," he added, feeling as he did so, that something wasn't quite right with what he'd just said.

Baby Kenneth wanted to go look, and, seeing as the rabbit wasn't too interested in the intellectual content of the story (now quickly dressing up as a lecture), Poorly Boy took him across to the window ledge, riding on the hyacinth shoulder-muffling hyena rug, which trailed on the floor as it was far too long for Poorly Boy.

He opened the curtains a little so the rabbit could cat-flap spot while warmly resting in the thermal hat Poorly Boy used when beds were short in the Garden Shed Infirmary.

"Asteroidal moggies" – the fairy and Nelly were wavy browed and frowning as Poorly Boy resumed his discourse- "like the toms, er, aren't striped either. Some are diamond patterned and some have noughts and crosses – gives them something to do when there's no meteoric mice to chase."

Nelly didn't look any more believing than she had earlier over her mother's returning from heaven with toys sometime in the future. Her trunk, like the rest of her, appeared to Poorly Boy to be turning a deeper, redder kind of pink.

"A story this might be if we stay up long enough, but it isn't true and you go telling us it is! We're not as easily taken in as young Kenneth."

Nelly he'd expected to give him the sharp edge of her trunk at any minute, judging by the colour it was going. He knew the telltale signs of old. But when the anticipated attack came from the fairy it found him wide-eyed, weakly smiling and, for once – if only for a brief once – lost for a response.

The fairy continued, poking her wand at Poorly Boy.

"You tell us the difference between a tom and a moggie from outer space and how they got into outer space, and for why and for what for?"

The ferocity of this wand-waving, tinselled, glaring onslaught on his honesty brought the slowly drawn out:

"Er, it's like this …"

And just then, as it so happened, just like that, Baby Kenneth called them to come over to the window that very second.

After a quick consultation with the baby blue rabbit, Poorly Boy fell over his trailing rug in his haste to collect Nelly and the fairy for a window-ledge observatory view of the mauve galactic flap just named Kenneth in honour of its discoverer.

"That is not mauve!" snapped Nelly.

"OK, clever, what colour is mauve?"

Poorly Boy himself was getting a little mad, smarting at being called not in so many words, but by hints, a fibber and maker-up of things.

"Mauve", she observed regally, "is mauve."

"And that up there is mauve," yelled baby Kenneth gleefully.

"Don't you go getting historical. It's bad at your age," advised Nelly. She went on patiently, getting angrier. "It's a dirty grey cloud coming to see if it ought to rain tomorrow. And what you think is a silly cat flap is a big hole through it."

"The hole the toms and moggies go through to other galaxies chasing fast mice!" spluttered Baby Kenneth, more hysteric than historic.

"You're so right, Baby Kenneth," agreed Poorly Boy, "and its mauve, just as you said it was."

At that, Nelly wet from deep pink to blueish purple and was on the verge of telling Poorly Boy what he knew already – that he didn't know what mauve was – when Pat started to put her tidying-up things away into the bag she had marked 'Property of Heaven' (the one with the official harp logo on the side).

She was ready to leave, everywhere being nice and tidy by now. At the door of the room in Poorly Boy's mind, she stopped and turned. Poorly Boy saw his other mother smile such a long smile and blow him such a kiss as he knew would be all sloppy like those she was always giving him in hospital. He felt it on his inner cheek and felt happy.

The fairy yawned and, as if their mouths were slow-motion dominoes in a slow-motion line, the others yawned.

"You're not worth arguing with, Poorly Boy," said Nelly, making her way over to bed.

"We girls will now go to sleep and leave those ridiculous children to their fairy stories," added the fairy. "I've got to catch a train back to the cupboard early in the morning. I'm not going to miss my holiday for those two."

Within less time than it takes to say 'asteroidal moggies' they were asleep.

"Poorly Boy," whispered Baby Kenneth, "shall we stay up and wait for the meteor mice to come through the flap, and watch them be chased by the toms with the adds and take-aways on them?"

"If you like," said Poorly Boy, lovingly snuggling up to Baby Kenneth beside the two sleeping girls on the pillow.

He gave the baby rabbit a big, sloppy, wet kiss on his nose. The blue into the black made a little mauve patch. Poorly Boy thought – could be.

The Lone Edward

Baby Kenneth had just shot Ben. He lay there moaning as Little Sheeps moved in to finish him off.

"Leave him alone, you wicked sheep! Back up! Drop your water pistol, Kenneth the Kid and, both of you, over to the wall with your paws and hoofs in the air."

"Shucks, Ranger Pee Bee," said Ben. "Am I pleased to see you?!"

"Don't talk now, Sherriff Dad," advised Poorly Boy. "I'll send Miss Nelly to get Doc Crumble Bee, and we'll have you mended faster than you can bleed to def!"

"Night-night, partner."

Ben kissed Poorly Boy and tucked Little Sheeps (who had by now been hung for murder and forgiven) in for the night. The big bad sheep's crafty black eyes reflected the crafty brown eyes of the Poorly Boy in the landing light through the open bedroom door, as both sets peered out from under the sheets. Poorly Boy, alias Ranger Pee Bee, turned from bright eyes catching bright eyes to cheek to cheek with the villainous sheep. Remembering his rangerly duties, Poorly Boy could now, with their heads both low on the pillow together, ensure Little Sheeps couldn't get up to any more naughtiness in the night. Baby Kenneth, alias Kenneth the Kid, was under the custody of Daddy Springy on the bedside cabinet, while awaiting trial the next day for shooting Ben, robbing the bank of lettuce in the garden, and leading Little Sheeps astray.

"Thanks, Dad, for playing the lone ranger and cow rabbits with us. Can I see the film again soon?"

"Of course you can, sweetheart!" said Sue from the doorway. "Maybe tomorrow evening after we come home from hospital."

The lone ranger had been a hero of Poorly Boy's ever since he first saw the DVD of the movie eight times ago.

Next day Poorly Boy was to go to for one of his periodic examinations. It was a simple routine appointment, which, like all such, would occupy most of the day. Poorly Boy knew many of the staff, it being the hospital to which he had originally been admitted with his heart condition.

To reach the clinic, Sue, Ben and Poorly Boy always went through the children's ward, visiting friends among nurses and stopping to talk with sick children. Toys were everywhere about their business, or resting from it. Lots were in one corner, where they lived in a variety of boxes. It was from here that the lone Edward and Tonto Pig would ride out on hand horses, day or night to save sick children from as much crying as possible.

The Lone Edward was presently with a small boy under attack from a band of ruthless tears, who were making him cry for his mother. It was the blind teddy bear's first mission of the morning. His faithful Red Indian pig, Tonto, wore his chief's headdress of plastic feathers, earned for some good deed or for which some girl rewarded him (actually off her brother's Red Indian brave soft-toy field mouse), was at that moment three beds away on the floor, where he had dropped bravely on his nose to make another poorly child giggle. The headdress rolled away into the ward – not surprisingly, as a field mouse is smaller than a pig and it was not an ideal fit. That child was now fast asleep, and Nurse resaddled in her hand Tonto Pig (minus headdress, which was somewhere else on the ward floor). He rode over to help the Lone Edward fight off the Heartless Tears Mob. Edward had no eyes, both having been lost at different times while defending children from heartache, fears and loneliness, but Tonto Pig went with him everywhere, or was never far away, and his eyes served them both.

A small boy, by now rescued from the renegade and always raiding Damp Cheeks Band, was happily talking to a nurse attending him.

There came drifting to the ears of Edward a voice he thought he recognised from out of the usual clatter and bustle of the Children's Ward – a voice from a time when he could see. The mouth that fitted the voice, and the face that belonged to it, he could see right now in the sacred album the Book of Memory holds of our lives.

"Tonto, do you hear that voice? Is it possibly the voice of him, the Poorly One, who once had a name like other children by which I knew him and I know him still but will never speak?" Why, it's as if I named and even gave birth to him myself, so close is he to me!"

Tonto Pig thought that this was going a bit far but didn't say so. Pig and Bear sat recovering from their saving efforts, between a boy's legs on top of a bed.

"I do believe it is the voice of the rider with the Poorly Heart, who was first brought to you and me when you were wickedly bear-napped from him by the Forces of Unhappiness, disguised as the naughty child who stole you, whose job it is to make good children weepful and miserable."

"Yes, and had it not been for you saving me when I turned up in the part of the hospital babies go to get weighed before they're born, I wouldn't be here now."

"Indeed no, you would not, Lone Edward. At that time I was working there and nursed you back to health and taught you the way of the Indian Hospital Pig, and the caring for children, and of how to ride the palms of doctors and nurses to get to the wild, West Children's ward, where next we were needed."

They fell silent, listening to the voices in the ward, Tonto Pig remembering he must retrieve his headdress as soon as possible. That was when the trusty Red Indian pig caught sight of Big Chief Poorly Heart. Once before had he seen him passing through the ward, wild because of the raw sound of children's joy and children's pain, when Lone Edward still had an eye and could point out to his faithful pig. Then, however, Lone Edward had been too weak from his recent bear-napping ordeal to even think of reuniting with the poorly boy without a name, let alone leaving hospital in his arms.

"No, we are wrong, Lone Edward. It is not the one – only a child who sounds like him, for all young children sound similar."

Tonto Pig felt ashamed of himself. He was lying to his beloved Lone Edward – for the best of reasons and the worst of reasons.

If Lone Edward knew Big Chief Poorly Heart had returned, would he want to go home with him and leave Tonto alone? He would then become just another sad soft toy amidst broken wheels and chocolate malted, matted nylon fur, sometimes needed and warm beside a child, but more often cold and forgotten on the floor. (This reminded him again he must get his headdress back.) The Pig lied because he could not take the chance of losing Lone Edward.

A cry of anguish rose from the bed or 'ranch bunk' nearest the doors, as the toy twosome called it. A little girl newly arrived the evening before was sobbing uncontrollably. Nurse smiled at the boy who owned the legs where the twosome rested, and she hand-rode the pair quickly to where the girl sobbed. A doctor and two nurses were already with her. As the two rode up, Big Chief Poorly Heart arrived at the scene also, on his way through the ward to some appointment elsewhere. He saw the twosome, and recognised them as of his own kind.

"Little girl," he said, standing by the bedside, doctors and nurses silently watching. "Don't you cry, for here are two brothers of mine, from the same tribe. These good friends can take away your cares and play with you till your mummy comes, for she is not far away."

Lone Edward was now even more certain he recognised that voice, as the voice's hands rode him and Tonto the last stage of the journey from nurse to little girl.

"This teddy bear here, he is so like the beloved one I once had and lost somewhere in this very hospital that it brings tears to my eyes. But mine are tears of joy, for I know that this teddy and his piggy friend will be to you as my toys are to me. My teddy had two eyes, but this one – the blind teddy who has ridden all these miles from that boy's bed four beds away – can see just as far into your heart, and follow and look after your every move, as my teddy did then and as my other toys do now."

The girl pressed the bear and the pig to her with such force that her glasses rose off her nose and ears and had to be rescued by the nurse.

"Do I know you, little girl?" asked Big Chief Poorly Heart.

"Is your name by any chance –"

"I don't think so!" It was a man's voice, deep and cheerful. "I don't think your name is that, unless the fairies have changed it overnight from Sue, which it was after we'd—"

"Kissed and gone to sleep," interrupted Sue after Ben had interrupted her.

"Yes, after we'd done that as well," added Ben with a mischievous look in his eyes, which Sue ignored.

"I think I've been dreaming," yawned Sue.

"I'm not surprised. You always get a bit uptight and anxious when we're going on hospital matters. Dream anything good, did you?"

"Not really." Sue was thoughtful, trying to recall details as she spoke. "It seemed pretty vivid when you woke me, but it's fading."

"It'd better fade even quicker, dear wife. We've got to be at the hospital for Pee Bee's appointment in an hour."

The three of them walked through the west-facing Children's ward together with Kenneth the Kid, who Poorly Boy claimed was proud of being an outlaw rabbit and was quite unafraid of being brought to trial for shooting Ben with an empty water pistol and rampaging round the kitchen with a carrot rifle stolen from Sue when she was getting the salad ready for tea. He was also proud of the only slightly lesser charge of not doing as Daddy Springy told him last night in going to bed without any supper for being a naughty young rabbit – unless he had two chocolate peanuts first, which he made sure he did.

As they approached the doors leading off the ward, to go through to the department they needed, Sue was not really surprised to see a girl about Poorly Boy's age wearing glasses. She reminded her of young Pat, the terminally ill child who'd grown so close to her son when he was in hospital the first time with his heart condition. She wasn't surprised, either, to see the girl playing with a battered and eyeless teddy and also what distinctly looked like a brown-and-white soft-toy pig.

Why she wasn't surprised she couldn't say. It was oddly a feeling more of relief than surprise when the Red Indian headdress she'd almost dreaded to see on the pig on the bed with girl and teddy was not there. The girl, the blind teddy and the pig were quite enough in themselves.

"Come on Mummy!" Poorly Boy called from the door, where Ben held his hand. "What have you stopped for?"

He freed himself from his father's grip and trotted over to Sue. Stooping, he picked something up close by her feet.

"This, belongs to that little girl's pig there, Mum. Isn't she a lot like Pat?"

On Suefari

Poorly Boy was at a loose end with no operations and no one to play with. Those children he knew were at school. He was too much at risk, so the people-doctors cautioned him against going there too. Any minute, they said, his poorly heart might look at the clock and decide it, and Poorly Boy, ought to be in hospital – or even elsewhere. They said 'elsewhere' very gravely whilst looking at Sue and Ben, who'd look at each other and look down.

Poorly Boy always looked up, however, at such moments. He wasn't going anywhere other than up, for he had so much to do – so much to make right in the garden, the street, the world; so many poorly toys to make smile again; so many children to give imaginations; so many people to give heart to, if not to heal.

Today was one of those days the sun keeps its arms folded though, and birds mutter more than sing upon. On days like this, fluffy, merry clouds can't be bothered and blue skies don't get up, but grey skies seem to like such days and rain clouds threaten to visit before supper. Poorly Boy knew it depended on him alone what the day would do, for in his short lifetime he'd often been left to make its mind up for it when others of its family members had been bored.

Poorly Boy also knew there was great risk attached to these decisions. Often he decided the day's fate would rest indoors with a TV set or colouring book, or enjoying hours spent irritating his mother. Often the day wouldn't take its medicine, though, and while he was refusing to eat his dinner it was out playing in the bright sunshine, defying his decision to stop indoors.

The palms of Poorly Boy's hand were philosophically contemplating these imponderables with his chin, at one particular loose end, just after breakfast. His elbow was gently rocking itself to sleep with his arm stood to attention on the window ledge, whilst with his chin on his palm a chorus of fingers tried to drum their personal opinion on either side of his nose. His eyes looked up and, as always, the sky was awaiting his directions. It was Nurse Nelly who made a suggestion suddenly as she entered the kitchen on the tray Sue was carrying.

"Why don't we go and hunt calories in the garden?" she said. "You know what days are. If we decide to stop in, and I spend it defending your Mum against you lot, it'll defy us and be nice and sunny while I'm struggling beside Mum against you and Little Sheeps in here. On the other hand, if we get our coats on and go on a calorie-hunting expedition, it'll either join us with a grin on its face or cry all over us. We'll just have to take our chances."

Just as Nelly finished, Sue, unbeknownst to herself, agreed.

"Why don't you put your coat on and go outside and risk it? It's grey, but not raining – and it'll be much greyer still if you stop in all day under my feet. So go on – wrap up and see if your play'll make the day grin!"

Poorly Boy stared at Nelly, startled by her skills as a ventriloquist. The tray landed gently like a flying saucer after doing a slow turn above the drainer.

That was it, then, adjudged his nose as it came down like a gavel. His chin and palm parted in agreement with the decision, fingers drumming them off with a brief march on his cheek, lasting but a second, before they did so.

"Right, Mum. Good idea – and seeing as it's yours, you can be boss of packing us up for what Nelly decided the other day would be a good idea next time we hadn't none and you had the idea we should have. I'll go and get some grass for sandwiches and you fill a bottle. Lemon, please – the team likes that as well, so we won't have to come back till we've caught one!"

This led to a few questions in Sue's mind. She was going to raise them, but she found herself about to address the open door to the garden. But Poorly Boy wasn't long gone, and Sue got another chance to raise them. She put the fresh grass cuttings (a mere three weeks old) between six slices of bread and margarine.

Little Sheeps and Daddy Springy don't like wet grass; if it's dry, you can damp some for Baby Kenneth's as he likes it soggy."

"Why am I doing this, Poorly Boy?" This was Sue's first and not unreasonable question.

Poorly Boy gave her the 'you must know' look, which we all use on people whose ignorance amazes us. He handed her, with scrupulously undried five-year-old washed/unwashed hands, another paw-load of yummy only-just-beginning-rotting compost off the table's edge, where he'd dumped it from the garden. The paws involved belonged to Little Sheeps and Daddy Springy.

"You're doing it. Mum, because Nelly, being a nurse, is wondering why all grown-ups and far too many bit-grown-ups are scared of calories. You are. You watch one every time you spot it on a box of eats as if it's going to eat you – and all them people on telly and on mag'ine pages do, counting every one they see. You're all afraid of them, and Nelly wants to find out why."

Sue all at once found herself giving the answer, but she was aware of doing it oddly, almost in a defensive panic:

"It's because they put weight on us – and weight where we don't want it."

She'd regrets even before the end of her answer. Poorly Boy had led her to the hunter's pit and shoved her in for Nelly – her staunchest ally, even before Ben – to desert her and put the net over Poorly Boy's pit. Sue started to squirm at the bottom of it as Poorly Boy stared one of his 'pity the poor fool' stares – first at Nelly, to see if she'd got the same stare as him, and then at Sue, who knew she was that poor fool waiting the pit's filling-in.

Poorly Boy commenced shovelling:

"Oh, Mum, me and Nelly's surprised you didn't think of it too – as well as us."

'Oh, God,' thought Sue, 'not the high chair!'

Now, this high chair dated back to Poorly Boy's babyhood – all those many five years. He'd never let Sue and Ben remove it from its domineering hold on the kitchen corner. At times of great danger to the nation – or when there was a threat to his pocket money for being naughty, or to the Garden Shed Infirmary, or to Baby Kenneth's tooth, or if there was a pending shortage of cottage cheese cartons – he'd pompously reinstate it at its head-of-table position. From here, swinging (just enough for effect but not enough to upend it) with one foot on the first rung and the other sort of dangling hypnotically in the air, he'd give an oration on whatever threat was impending.

"You can't blame the calories – that's one thing."

Sue interrupted bravely here, attempting to suppress the next shovelful.

"I'm well aware of that Poorly Boy; it's we who tend to eat too many of them."

Her voice was rather lacking patience, whereas Poorly Boy was still patiently talking as though to a fool in the pit, his leg still beating air like a subdued tom-tom before the cook pot Sue was about to face. The assembled team, less Nelly, assembled on the high-chair tray before her (Nelly was still undecided about whether to get Sue out or join the cannibals); Poorly Boy then dragged Sue firewood-wards.

"Mummy, Mummy," he began, "if you know you eat too many, why do it? Why do it when you know it only gets them even madder and they'll scare you even more?"

Sue, cowering in the pit bottom, looked at him, expressionless.

"They aren't nasty – born that way. Oh no, it's because you and all them people who eat calories get 'em real uptight because you eat them. If you leave them alone and eat proper food instead, leaving the little calories to get on and eat whatever calories eat, they can too have a happy time of their lives and have babies and get married after, just like what we do."

By this time Sue was almost pleased to give up the fight and throw herself into the cook pot – so she did.

"But, Poorly Boy, all food contains calories. Only water has none."

"That's because they can't swim, Mum. In fact, there's a starting for you because you can teach them. Just smile and say, 'Look – we know we've been cruel to you all these years, but now we isn't going to hurt you poor fings no more; and to prove it we will show you how to doggy-paddle and not be put off by water any more or have to go the long way round puddles.' Think about it, Mum."

Sue was. It was getting hotter and hotter. She remembered her school day science – a bit – and how a calorie was a sort of measure. (She recalled something about raising temperature through one gram of water for some obscure reason – or was it how to raise one gram to the water's surface? Whatever! She did know they could be fattening if you ate too many, and all food and drink contained them, other than water because they couldn't swim.) She realised her head ached and she was becoming a little confused.

Poorly Boy put more wood on the cooking fire.

"They're in the food, Mum, 'cos they dig wiv their sharp teeth a way in to try escaping from you. They dun't want to fight because they're only small – so small you need a microscope to see them bigger than what they are – but they are very brave for their size. If you touch them in nastiness it's only nat'ral they'll bite back, isn't it? That brings me back to where I started."

Sue felt she might be about done on both sides. All that remained, then, was for Poorly Boy to start carving.

"Leave them alone, Mum – that's my advice to you and all who hurts 'em out there – and then you won't even notice they're about."

Poorly Boy left off swinging from the judgement chair and one-legged it across to the compost sandwiches.

"Take this, Mum." His tone was biblical and 'all sermons on the rocks'. "See," he said with a flourishing hand, "it dun't bite because there's no calories around it. They knew all along Little Sheeps and Daddy Springy weren't going to hurt them; and, now I've teached you, you won't neither hurt them. They sense it, see, Mum. So when they'd finished playing on the grass and the bread (those who ha'n't already jumped off when you chopped and margarined), they skipped off hand in hand and singing so sweet you can't hear them, to play elsewhere. They didn't need to hide inside the bread or grass by burrowing through the surface wiv those same teeth you used to be – before today – scared stiff of. Do you understand now how silly you've been, Mummy?"

Nelly unexpectedly fell forwards into some milk Poorly Boy had spilt on the tray, seemingly days before at breakfast. Though this was small comfort to Sue, who felt her pink be-trunked saviour had arrived too late, at last what was left of her might still be pulled free, out of the pot, by the young elephantess.

"Well, Nelly for one obviously doesn't agree with you, Poorly Boy. She's just seen a calorie about to attack her, and maybe, even me, in that split milk there and has jumped on it to squash it!" Sue felt better for this – if only for a moment.

Poorly Boy righted Nelly – unduly roughly, thought Sue.

"Not at all," he said after a moment's contemplation of the scene before him.

Sue saw his brain's brainwave cheerfully waving at her from the glittering windows of Poorly Boy's brown eyes.

"No, Mum – wrong again! Nelly's turned thirsty wiv all your talking – and she's not scared of calories neither. She knows there won't be any hiding from her in that milk and they'll all have gone off playing safely from round it when they saw she's thirsty. They'll work wiv you if you work wiv them."

Everyone heard the day make up its mind for itself: it rained heavily because it thought no one was interested in a calorie hunt outside; so Poorly Boy called the whole thing off. Leaving Little Sheeps and Daddy Springy to eat their tasty sandwiches on the table, after the safari and the hunting expedition just successfully carried out he decided to help Sue wash up the pots from breakfast.

"Look at this porridge pan!" he giggled. "It's gone all messy wiv leaving too long. It looks as if some – what do you call them? – oh, cannonballs or somefing's been cooking calories in it. I wonder if they found them fattening, Mum!"

There came to Sue's imagination the image of a friendly little savage grinning up at her.

The Big Nudge

Things had a way of falling into Poorly Boy's hand because Poorly Boy nudged them. He was out nudging hands, trotting across the car park in the centre of town one afternoon whilst holding Sue's hand. Nelly's words were ringing for possible nudges to his imagination.

"Crumble Bee can't play forward centre or go on striker because he's too important a bee for football, and he's too many legs for one ball. He wouldn't know which to kick it with." She'd claimed.

Though Little Sheeps had suggested Crumble Bee play in goal, his eleven and a half legs being ideal for the position, Nelly had disdainfully told him to go play there himself, stupid sheep that he was.

"Mr Crumble Bee will not be kicking balls about," she affirmed, trunkily and finally.

That left Poorly Boy short of not only four players none of the team wanted to be, but the fifth one as well for the five-a-side team to play Uncle Peter's Floppy Duck, Granny Gip and Mr Donkle, on transfer loan from Tiny. Floppy Duck being massive, it was decided to count him as two players. The game was to be played that night under floodlights at Tiny's Tabletop Stadium in her kitchen. Poorly Boy had to get nudging fast.

Mum was at that moment dragging him more than trotting him reluctantly from the Doctor's surgery, where she'd been to have an eye infection looked at, back to Uncle Peter's car, which was waiting in the car park.

"Come on Poorly Boy – why do you drag your arm so? Uncle Peter's only got lunch, then he's at work again!"

Poorly Boy was looking around him as if he'd a prior engagement with a friendly nudge.

In fact he had, for the day before, after the Doctor had prescribed treatment for the eye, telling Sue to come back the following day, Poorly Boy noticed a nudge that now, twenty-four hours later and in the absence of any more nudges turning up, could be made to drop into his hand. Upon first seeing it the day before, he'd made a fuss and carried on dragging at Mum's arm to such an extent that she let go of his hand, telling him to either follow her or stay in the car park while she got on the bus at the station next to it. Poorly Boy had followed sulkily behind, of course – but now it was time for him to really nudge the issue.

"There he is again, Mum. Poor, poor rabbit – just where he was yesterday, only wetter, sadder, and more in need of a good football team than ever!"

"I told you: that is not coming home! It's a dirty, disease-ridden old toy nobody but you would want. I caved in over Crumble Bee, but you're not taking that home, yesterday, today, or a Christmas twelve years from now!" Briefly she wondered why she'd said that last of all.

Poorly Boy petulantly shook his hand free and stood his little bit of ground while he prepared for the Big Nudge. Putting his hands together in the time-honoured, endearingly sweet, angelic-child-attempting-to-get-his-own-crafty-way pose, he started.

"Mummy, last night when I told Daddy Springy about us seeing Sad Rabbit all alone and no one loving him or calling him by a special name in this car park or in the whole world, he said it was his long-lost brother Reg. He said he hadn't seen him since they last played football together."

Mum couldn't believe it – Poorly Boy was resorting to such a daft tale. Where were his legendary powers of imagination and invention? Could she really be hearing such a lame story from her son?

Unexpectedly Poorly Boy raised both arms skywards from the prayer position, like a preacher invoking God, only it wasn't the Almighty he invoked but Uncle Peter, who, almost as if at a prearranged signal, got out of his car a few parked vehicles away and ran across to them. Sue fleetingly felt suspicious – but surely not! She dismissed it – after all, whatever reason could there possibly be for suspicion? What could be the object of a plot, pray? Nevertheless she had an unaccountable sinking feeling.

"There he is, Uncle Peter," said Poorly Boy, pointing to where the rabbit was just being run over by departing wheels of a car. "Him what's just been squished," he added, voice and face expressionless.

Uncle Peter raised a hand to shade his brow.

'Quite unnecessarily theatrical!' thought Sue, as the rain started to fall from the sky, which had been without sun for days.

"Is that Daddy Springy's brother, Poorly Boy?" said Sue's younger brother, in his best Rabbit De Niro voice. "Oh yes, I can see he's both a Springy and a striker rabbit of great potential, just like Daddy Springy told you, Poorly Boy, when you were at my house last evening."

Sue acknowledged to herself that she'd been incorrect in allowing Poorly Boy and her brother the benefit of the doubt.

"Listen, you couple of apes," she said (reasonably, under the circumstances). "Do you think I'm stupid?"

"No, Mum," replied Poorly Boy after a hurtful, rather too long delay in thinking about it. "I just think you're a bit tired and you've forgotten me and Uncle Peter isn't apes but your boy and his uncle."

Sue glared at Uncle Peter.

"I'm ashamed to call you brother," she said.

"Try it – it's better than ape," suggested Uncle Peter.

Crumble Bee had originally been taken home in a plastic bag held under Poorly Boy's pushchair. Because he was found in the street, dirty and discarded. Mum wouldn't allow him to be taken home any other way. She'd never allowed Crumble Bee in the house. It was now Reg's turn to come in from the tarmac and find sanctuary with Poorly Boy by travelling there in the boot of Uncle Peter's car.

The reunion between Daddy Spring and Reg Springy was a cheerless affair in the Garden Shed Infirmary, unattended by either Sue or Uncle Peter, who were at the time involved in a heated argument about footballing rabbits and related concerns back at the house. Daddy Springy, however, did rather like the feel of the see-through plastic glove Sue had made Poorly Boy wear to handle Reg. He told Poorly Boy he wouldn't mind one of them for sleeping in on top of Poorly Boy's bedside cabinet at night. It would make an ideal sleeping bag – hygienic and easily washed.

"It's good to see you, Rolly," said an either tearful or just wet Reg Springy.

"Please don't call me that," requested a rather subdued, even surly, Daddy Springy.

"Aw, don't worry Rolly!" said Little Sheeps, more sarcastically than sympathetically. "Your brother is a great footballer, and I won't ever call you Rolly if you pay me enough."

"Is your brother staying?" asked Nelly whilst stifling chuckles in the time-honoured, soft-toy, pink-elephant way of turning vivid crimson in ears and trunk.

"I'm going to live here, Nelly," Reg Springy assured her.

"Er, not here as such," corrected Poorly Boy. "Tiny wants a rabbit – I hope – and she would love Daddy Springy's brother to live with her."

The football match didn't take place that evening, as Uncle Peter unexpectedly had to hurry away somewhere during his row with Sue at the house. Sue was only too pleased to get a chance to stop shaking with rage and go out, wheeling Poorly Boy's pushchair. At his suggestion they went round to Tiny's with Reg Springy held down the side and under the chair in a plastic bag. It wasn't far and Poorly Boy most times could have walked, but recently he'd been unwell with his poorly heart – that heart which at all times worried them and sometimes terrified them. However, it was late summer, and even though it was constantly overcast the rain dried quickly on clothing as if the hidden sun felt guilty. Part way to Tiny's it started to shower heavily, and they sheltered under a bus-stop canopy.

"Why, when I offered to buy you a new soft-toy rabbit, did you insist on this dreadful thing?"

"You know me, Mum," replied Poorly Boy. "Anyway, Tiny's mum's got her into computers and them electric games, and I'm frightened she'll forget the simple and soft and go the way of the hard screen."

The rain sizzled the silence to a ready-cooked heartache, and Sue looked away through a misty shelter with misty eyes.

Neither Daddy Springy, once out of Sue's handbag where he'd travelled to Tiny's, nor Reg Springy could give a reason why they'd been separated all those years. Poorly Boy thought it was because Daddy Springy had been a rabbit who wanted to follow books and learning, whilst his brother had wanted to go after the power of the mind to make pictures. That meant leaving home and travelling about, living the life of a tramp rabbit. Tiny didn't seem too keen on Daddy Springy's brother. She didn't like tramps much, but because she hated to hurt Poorly Boy she only told him she hated Reg Springy with her eyes. Poorly Boy was too good at listening to eyes to be fooled.

"So," said Nelly, "no football-match because Uncle Peter and your mum have fallen out over Reg here and he's gone off in a temper! No getting a good home for Reg because Tiny didn't want him! He isn't going to settle in a house anyway because he's already told us toys he's been 'on the road', as he puts it, so long he can't stay indoors long. And no way can he stay here in the Garden Shed Infirmary with us – even if he could stay indoors – because I won't let him!"

Poorly Boy's plastic mac was longer than he was, and it trailed mini-magicians-cloak-like in the long wet grass beside the road.

"It's as Reg says. Uncle Peter: He won't ever go hungry 'cos of the carrot he's always had between his paws since he was born."

"That's another reason he does so well on the roads, is it, Poorly Boy?" replied Uncle Peter as he led Poorly Boy by the hand along the verge at the side of a quiet country road.

"This is the place, Uncle Peter, where he said he wanted leaving."

Poorly Boy knelt and placed Reg Springy part under the gorse hedge and part in the long grass that, as he knelt there, reached up well over Poorly Boy's shoulders. Rabbit and boy were for a moment greenly swathed, safely away from the road.

They returned to the car and began to eat sandwiches.

"Reg wasn't really Daddy Springy's proper brother, Uncle Peter, you know," said Poorly Boy as he rummaged down at his feet for the ham out of his sandwich. "All soft-toy boy rabbits call each other Reg or Rolly. They ain't got no other first names but those when they're born, and the only second name they all have is Springy. The girl rabbits' second name is always Leapy."

"Tell me more – sound confusing," said Uncle Peter, washing a banana down with a canned drink.

"Not when they've found a home with a little boy or girl, Uncle Peter. That's when they get their proper names, like Daddy Springy got 'Daddy' which of course he is to Baby Kenneth."

"So, all soft-toy rabbits are either brothers or sisters because they're of the same species – that it, Poorly Boy?"

"No, they're of the same soft-toy rabbits, Uncle Peter."

Uncle Peter didn't argue; he only pondered to himself about what two first names the females went by.

"Why didn't Reg want to stay with us?"

Uncle Peter handed Poorly Boy a tissue to wipe his hands.

"Because no one wanted him, Uncle Peter. Mum didn't, Tiny didn't; even Nelly let him know he wasn't wanted."

"Wouldn't have got on with your Floppy Duck, Uncle Peter. Nobody does." Poorly Boy finished clumsily wiping his hands, and his beautiful brown eyes enfolded his uncle's. "There's homeless toys everywhere, Uncle Peter. Most of them were never loved enough to be named in a child's mind pictures. I saw Reg alone and unwanted, and I gave him the chance of a home with a roof; but, unlike other toys, he didn't want to be owned in a child's world in the head. He also saw that Tiny is losing her own inner pictures to a silly electric screen's pictures. He didn't want that kind of world. He only feels safe in car parks and down grassy lanes, where he can be with the birds and flowers – part of the living world's true paintings. He's safe now and happy in his own world of whatever happens – car wheels or cowsheds."

The enfolding brown eyes let Uncle Peter's gaze free from their enchantment. They looked out through the windscreen at the soft summer rain nudging drops slowly down the glass.

"Who's going to play in goal if we ever get to have our football match, Poorly Boy?"

"Crumble Bee, of course, Uncle Peter. Look – I've found the middle of my sandwich; you're sat on it and its tongue's sticking out at me!"

Poorly Boy playfully gave his uncle a little nudge.

Another Hoof Up

It was Little Sheeps who found it and brought it to the attention of Poorly Boy, who picked it up and put it with the other three in the bottom drawer in his bedroom. Frowning, he wrapped it carefully with them, closed the door and, deeply pondering, went back to the Garden Shed Infirmary.

"Have a look at that sack over in the corner, Poorly Boy. I think it's empty, so throw it on the pile."

Mr Brown was cleaning out his allotment hut, and the rubbish he and Poorly Boy had ousted made an odd assortment of buckled never-seen-anything-like-its and broken what's-this-for-Mr-Brown? Poorly Boy dived into the friendly shadows dripping cobweb clothes lines and came out a little shuffling scuttling later dragging the bottom corner of a heavy sack. Pushing bottom lip over top, he blew some spider-silk garment, left there from the clothes lines, off it and up his nose like an eight-leg-spun handkerchief.

"There's somebody in it, Mr Brown," said Poorly Boy excitedly. "I fink it's a baby badger hiding from his mummy, who wants a word with him about muckying her clean bathroom towel!"

"You reckon!" laughed the lonely old man, who laughed these days only when the sun shone – fittingly disguised as Poorly Boy's face.

"You've got to be joking!" exclaimed Sue.

Poorly Boy felt he'd done enough being angelic for one day; he decided to be awkward instead – or so it seemed. This was really nothing new. When he was awkward-seeming, he was actually in quite a reasonable mood – he was never obstreperous except for that worthy cause called 'Poorly Boy's take on life'.

"As a king, he needs a throne – and you tell me what he can use if he dun't use this bowl, which is just right for his royal bum."

"It's your great-great-grandmother's china milk jug, Poorly Boy, and that means it's not designed for being a throne – especially when the king happens to be a filthy, wrinkled, sprouty-everywhere old 'tato Mr Brown told you to throw away."

"But Mr Brown didn't realise King Edward was in the sack, Mummy. King Edward, MUM! Not just any cold mashed potato, but an actual *KING*." The awe in Poorly Boy's voice was just that – more awful than laudable.

Sue knew this meant he was earnest about his cause – it was one of his Poorly Boy visions for a world perfected along Poorly Boy lines. She waited and, as always, it came – one of those wide-eyed, winningly winsome, thoroughly disreputable, totally credible reasonings laid out for the benefit of idiots, which Poorly Boy specialised in passing off as explanations.

"If you follow me into the front room ..." suggested Poorly Boy.

Sue had the impression of a defence counsel about to ask a jury to accompany him for a tour of the dreadfully bleak wing which a life prisoner – should they so cruelly and misguidedly sentence his poor innocent client – would have to serve out his time upon. 'Pee Bee gathering the violets of sympathy' Ben had long ago termed it.

Sue rose and went with the young lawyer.

"In't he lovely, Mum! He's King Edward's pet."

Sue walked around the pet cautiously as it lay ready to do something or other in the middle of her great-grandmother's salver (likewise antique) in the centre of the table.

"Why is it there?" said Sue.

"Because it's waiting for the four whiskers and Baby Kenneth and his pet family to arrive wiv Daddy Springy."

It was possible to remonstrate, argue even and assert one's parental authority, but Sue was hooked and intrigued by the four whiskers and, of course, Baby Kenneth's family. She was about to say something – anything – when Poorly Boy resumed his learned defence of the indefensible.

"Watch the pet, Mummy, while I go upstairs and get them out of my drawer. Then you can go on watching him while I fetch Neville, Sandra and Baby Kenneth. Then you can go and get Daddy Springy while me and Little Sheeps over on the sideboard keep guard on them all for you. Sit down, Mum. Rest your toes."

Solicitously the five-year-old attorney pulled up a dining chair and dug it into the back of Sue's knees so she sat involuntarily down.

He wasn't gone long, and on his return he placed a pair of underpants beside the pet on the salver.

"You're not going to put them on it!"

"No – course not," Poorly Boy replied to this ridiculous accusation. "The whiskers is in it, silly."

Sue sat down again, realising she should have known this.

Poorly Boy left once more, going outside this time. Upon his return he put Baby Kenneth, Neville and Sandra on the salver – but not Jimmy, as he was still a baby and asleep after his dinner. This done, he stood back to survey the crowded plate. Then he looked about for a place to put the cardboard box he'd brought them in, and found Mum's lap.

"What are that small pink pig and the yellow rabbit for, Poorly Boy?" enquired Sue, flat-voiced with little tonal modulation.

"They is Baby Kenneth's family, Mum – his very own team of daddies and mummies to help him bring up Jimmy Rabbit, his plastic Christmas-cracker pet, who you've met millions of times."

Sue tried another tack up the road of Poorly Boy's raging imagination.

"What whiskers are in your Captain Wombat underpants?"

Poorly Boy's feverish grin left like the shadows, returning to Mr Brown whenever Poorly Boy went home again. He spoke darkly, concerned and serious.

"Little Sheeps found the first one on the concrete outside the front door where the post-lady slipped last winter and Dad had to carry her in and you got on to him when she left, when they sent a van for her for spraining her ankle, because you said Dad was a bit too quick to pick her up when she did it instead of waiting to see if she could stand –."

"Get on with it!" interrupted Sue, still very much monochrome.

"If you shut up and stop interpring, I will," suggested Poorly Boy. "Well," he continued, that being one whole sentence, which he made last, dragging out each letter as if he was milking it for import. "Well," he said again, pulling each of the word's four treats as Sue sighed like all the neighbourhood's cares sighing at once, "that's where Little Sheeps found it."

"What?"

"The first of Daddy Springy's whiskers wiv the other three at the back where you used to put Felix's food dish until I got tired of telling him to share his Goodibits wiv the starlings and not be so selfish; and you said you'd start to feed him inside the back door and give the starlings Goodibits in a dish of their own on top of the wall, where Felix was too fat to go. Well, you did for a start until you found out Goodibits is bad for birds as all the salt in them makes their feathers fall out."

"I never said that!" retaliated Sue.

A heated argument ensued, the ramifications of which need not detain us, other than to say that it lasted a half-hour and ended with both parties staring moodily at the salver in hot silence. Sue left without a word to fetch Daddy Springy from the Garden Shed Infirmary.

"I've not got time to fall out with you," announced Poorly Boy after some five further minutes of even more heated silent debate upon her return and overemphasised placing of the elder rabbit on what space remained on the salver. Poorly Boy got off the floor where he'd been semi-lotus-pose brooding, shrugged and unfolded the Captain Wombat underpants.

"Why have you got four bristles from the yard broom in there, Poorly Boy?" Sue asked in dread. It was only now that she understood why Poorly Boy had started combing Daddy Springy's white whiskers studiously with her hairbrush.

It took some while for Sue to persuade her son that soft-toy-rabbit whiskers neither grow nor turn black on falling out. He took no small convincing that it wasn't actually necessary for a potato called King Edward to bring along his pet spider with the special powers – the one on the salver with the white dangly legs sticking out of it (a bit like rabbit whiskers). Yet he just had to know. It was as if some powerful force was actually compelling her – against her nosy will, even – to find out what the rest of the entourage were doing on the salver, and what dark purpose really lurked behind the ritualistic involvement of her dear, dead great-grandmother's things.

"It's easy!" bounded Poorly Boy verbally forwards. "Mr Brown likes me, and baby Kenneth even more than me. He buys Neville Rabbit and Sandra Pig for him and gives them us this morning. They are new life, Mum. The three sprouty groups of crowns King Edward's got make him King of Growing Things – and if you plant him and his spider with all those whiskery legs, you'll have lots of prince and princess spuds and little spiderlet spudlings and tiny white potato flowers before you can say 'His Royal Majestic'. So you put the new life of Neville and Sandra together with their young rabbit owner, Baby Kenneth, and King Edward's spider – then you'll get new whiskers growing on old rabbits, like Daddy Springy. That's how it works, Mum," Poorly Boy rounded off with a flourish.

Sue had to know more. Poorly Boy's mind spun webs from scuttling brain cells, and they tended to catch the listener every time.

"Who told you all that, and who said involve your great-great-grandmother's family heirlooms?"

"We ain't used my massive grandmother's air-brooms; I used your hairbrush on Daddy Springy, and it was our yard brush the four whiskers came off, so you say, so I never touched her broom at all." His eyes grew large and glassy, like someone breathing on cold windows and writing 'idea' across. "What a great idea, though, that was! Why don't we do it today, Mum, when there's talk about the dirty way we poison the world's air every time you put on children's telly?" And then – in the sparking of those connections that ignite the lights that twinkle within us till about age ten, when Christmas morning becomes heavy afternoon after Christmas lunch – there came the flashing inevitability of it.

"Mummy! We've got massive grandmother's crockery from China and her silver for the meat. If we've still got her air-broom anywhere, I'll tidy up this stuff on the table and take that cardboard box off the floor, just like a good boy, and go outside while it's fine to brush some air down in the garden for you. Ain't I a thoughtful little-little boy, Mum?"

It wasn't until late that night, long after he'd gone with a new dishcloth and a bowl of water 'to wash the air's face with', that the truth behind his great-great-grandmother's involvement became clear to Little Sheeps if not to Sue.

"Before we go to sleep I've been dyeing my white fleece red to have a go at you," said the irate woolly one to Poorly Boy.

"I'm so sleepy, Little Sheeps, after planting the King and his pet near my pet underground ground so they can grow and link life wiv death again, and dead pets with grass and princesses growing. And the air in our garden had such a mucky face, and its mouth stretches from the front gate to the back fence!"

"I know it does!" declared a sheep on the point of turning simple irate into compound irritation. "I had to go up and down with your rusty old toothbrush doing its teeth, and it's a long way for a little sheep with bad knees from you breaking them that time. I felt plain daft doing it!"

"You won't let me forget your silly legs, will you?" mumbled poorly Boy. "Anyway, you was on the ladder of my hand when you did the teeth, so you didn't have to reach up. And the teeth were big, so you didn't have to peer around up there looking for them. You didn't have to stretch or anything, did you? I saved you any of all that."

Little Sheeps changed tack on this fruitless stretch of verbal water as Sue had earlier in the day.

"Why is it, when Daddy Springy and me told you all along those were yard-broom bristles, you still went ahead with that nonsense in the house?"

Poorly Boy snuggled up closer to his woolly mate on the pillow so that snub nose touched stitched one. They gazed cross-eyed into each other's souls.

"Cos I've been looking for an excuse to get great-great-massive-grandmother's things out – just so's we could remind the surroundings about her and let the past know we hadn't forgotten it. It must get very lonely – people always moving out of it, into the present, into the future, into memories."

"That's beautiful," said Little Sheeps after a moment's meditation.

"Yes, isn't it?" agreed Poorly Boy, whose eyes were hurting from being crossed and staring and tired. "And the best way to remind yesterday about itself is to put it nose to nose wiv the present," he continued.

"So that's why Baby Kenneth's lot were there – with them all being new or young, and King Edward and his spider kind of linking and sprouting the past into the future and the future into the past.

"That's right, Little Sheeps."

As Poorly Boy concurred, one eye dropped shut; and as it did so, Little Sheeps must have shut both his in a hurry, for he rolled off the pillow and under the bedclothes.

"I must have fell off suddenly!" Surprise was all over Little Sheeps' voice as Poorly Boy helped him up on board the pillow.

"If only every hand or paw or claw had a hand or paw or claw to pull it safely free from trouble come bedtime!" Poorly Boy's eyes were closed as he sighed those words.

Little Sheeps' were both open.

"If only the past handed just safe and good things to the present and future and none of the unsafe things!" replied Little Sheeps.

"If only hands would take hold of just the past's good things, and plant them once more in the present to grow out of them better futures for hands, claws, paws insects and Crumble Bee's dangles everywhere!" Poorly Boy's eyes were wide open too as he spoke lovingly, slowly, wistfully into those of Little Sheeps. Then there was silence, until a sleepy moment or fifty later he remarked, "And potatoes," just as Little Sheeps fell off for a second time.

Poorly Boy gave him another hoof up.

Amma and the Elephant

The mysterious old lady made her way towards Poorly Boy's front gate, along Poorly Boy's street, as she did at the same time every morning. She was watchful, Poorly Boy, meanwhile, this particular morning was watching telly the drought-and-war-torn African people during the current crisis. He was watching the time also, so that it could tell Uncle Peter when it would allow his nephew to go outside and greet the always darkly dressed old lady by the gate.

"Ok, nuisance, you can stop pestering and go now. God knows who she is and wherever she's started to appear from this last couple of weeks."

"Don't know neither. Ouch!" replied Poorly Boy, falling over something which wasn't there and bumping his and Nurse Nelly's knees against Uncle Peter's chair in his haste to get to the garden gate.

"We've been watching the place wiv no water on TV, Mrs Lady – all the team as usual, and Nelly as well as Uncle Peter, who's looking after us today while Dad 'n' Mum take Joan from next door to see her sick sister, who lives miles away. Uncle Peter is doing as he thinks is right and is sending money monthly to a little girl called Amma, who I've seen a picture of. His friend at work sent money first to her, but he can't no more 'cos his wife's run off with somebody who wanted to run off wiv her, so he's got to stop home and look after the little baby she left behind. Not good is it?" he commented, frowning.

The old lady smiled as she leant against the gate, catching her breath. Poorly Boy perched on his side of the gate on the 'bird ledge', as he called the wooden crosspiece at the bottom. He had a hand upon the woman's dark sleeve, whilst the other hand helped squash Nelly against the top of the gate to stop him falling.

"Uncle Peter wants to know why we never see you go home in the evening, Mrs Dark Lady. Mum and Dad haven't seen you go past neither, and the team and me every night till bedtime keep coming in the wheelbarrow/ambulance to look for you."

A surprisingly unlined and clear-complexioned face for one so aged kissed Poorly Boy's forehead.

"Oh, I come back all right, young man," she chuckled.

The light was on beside Poorly Boy's bed that night. Little Sheeps was on the window ledge after Poorly Boy had parted the curtains for him, as he always did after Sue, Ben or Uncle Peter this time had closed them.

"There she goes, just as I told you. 'Tain't no mystery unless catching a bus is mysterious, which it certainly wasn't when I used to catch one into town, from the field to the finch-'n'-chip shop, on a Friday."

"Finch 'n' chips! Exclaimed Poorly Boy. "Battered, I suppose?"

"'Course," answered Little Sheeps. "What did you think I was, Poorly Boy – a cannonball?"

Poorly Boy got out of bed and closed the curtains before Uncle Peter arrived to kiss everyone goodnight. He took Little Sheeps – still giggling away on the window ledge at the brilliance of his own fleecy wit – and went back to bed, where the team (minus Crumble Bee, of course) were on the pillow.

Crumble Bee was never allowed inside the house. Sue was adamant about it because Crumble Bee smelled dreadful. Found by Poorly Boy in the street, Crumble Bee's bedraggled origins precluded any visits to the house. Tonight, however, Crumble Bee was inside the house on Poorly Boy's bedside cabinet, purple resplendent beneath the lampshade – but he was allowed no nearer, because he smelled dreadful.

Poorly Boy settled his head into the softness, Daddy Springy and Baby Kenneth sharing it with him on one side of his face, Nelly and Little Sheeps on the other.

"There's something mysterious about that old lady, Little Sheeps, no matter what you say," argued Nelly. "Why is it that every day she insists on me being there to greet her with

Poorly Boy? And why does she hug and kiss me before we wave bye-bye to her? Tell me that, then."

"Little Sheeps turned towards Nelly, and Poorly Boy turned on the pillow to face Little Sheeps and Nelly's pink back; but it was Daddy Springy who answered from the other side away from them. Poorly Boy turned back in the bed to face him, allowing Little Sheeps and Nelly to slip down the pillow to cover themselves in blankets while still listening, because they felt cold.

"Prepare yourself, Nelly," intoned the sage rabbit.

Nelly did so. She covered her head by sliding further down as Poorly Boy fidgeted. She and Little Sheeps still listened.

"I believe the old lady is your mummy's granny. She has traced you through the hospital staff and by speaking to your mummy's mummy.

"Never!"

Poorly Boy whipped round in bed to give Little Sheeps a hoof up, away from the covers, it being obvious he didn't agree with Daddy Springy. He never agreed with anyone – including himself.

"Why would an old lady turn out every morning to hug an itsy-bitsy soft toy who once belonged to her grandchild, Pat, who died in hospital and was Poorly Boy's mummy whilst he was there? She could get a much better elephant, with batteries, with her pension, if she wanted."

Nelly, who was as tough as pink nails, started to weep – as she did always whenever her mother, Pat, was mentioned. Nelly was close to Crumble Bee as only a male bee and female elephant can be, so Poorly Boy put her close to Crumble Bee on the cabinet so that he could comfort her with his broken dangly.

The bedroom door opened and Uncle Peter came in to kiss everyone goodnight.

"Ho ho! I'm going to tell on you, Poorly Boy, me lad. You've got Crumble Bee in the house, and he's not welcome in town, is he now?"

Uncle Peter drew up a chair and Poorly Boy giggled. He pretended to push his nephew's head under the bedclothes, and the team raced down the pillow to save the neck of their beloved leader. With order restored, Poorly Boy asked Uncle Peter if he'd like to stay while they said their bedtime prayers.

"Oh, you mean your wish list for toys you want us to buy you – with God's help, of course?"

"No, no, no – be serious, Uncle Peter. We do that one in the morning, before we get up. I mean our night-time prayer for the world to turn round, get angry wiv everyone and yell at them to love one another, like Crumble Bee loves Nelly, protecting her from the heat of the lamp bulb (which is like the sun burning the poor people's crops) and comforting her with his dangly which is like the rich comforting the starving and those hurt by wars and hurt by men and women wanting bigger and bigger cars on smaller and smaller roads, getting more 'n' more clogged up with all the useless stuff the rich buy to throw away because they fink what makes a big man 'n' a big woman is the size of the rich things they dangle in front of the world, saying, 'Look at me! How important I am! I've got a red button on my remote and you haven't.) What really makes a man and woman big is when they themselves are poor, yet share their poor broken dangly with someone who hasn't even got that much to dangle of their own."

Uncle Peter, who didn't have a red button, thought it best after all that, he did stay for prayers. It would be interesting to hear what came next.

"Ok, Uncle Peter, you start," came next.

Meanwhile the old lady was at home. After getting off the bus, she had no fear of being mugged on the short distance from the stop. She had no fear. She had lived a very long life, seen one great war after another, and knew that they were all great wars. She had watched her husband die, her son and Pat, her granddaughter. She had watched the well off watch the poor, then press red buttons for aid to flow to ease their consciences, then press the red buttons to change channels back again to what first helped to make the poor poor, as soon as their consciences were eased. Her own youngest daughter had told how her dying child, Pat, had given her beloved toy elephant, Nelly, to Poorly Boy to look after, and how she had told Nelly to look after Poorly Boy.

So the old lady, who had Poorly Boy's address from her daughter, had taken Pat's old bedroom temporarily in her daughter's house – a longish bus ride away from the boy. She wanted to see the pink elephant and the boy entrusted with the mission her granddaughter had given him, and she wanted to see for herself whether he was fulfilling it, in his own little way. Bah! She admitted to herself that she was also curious as to the outcome of something her darling granddaughter had left behind: a job for a poorly lad and his elephant to do that in some way pointed towards the dawning of a young girl's independent spirit.

It was a thing she'd done and decided upon in her final days on earth – a thing that owed nothing to her parents' influence or her grandmother's. Yes, indeed – the old lady was very curious. She smiled to herself. The lad seemed to be doing pretty well despite his own ill health. She could just imagine him saying that one final prayer he'd confided to her by the gate – a wish that God would make it possible for Amma somewhere caught up in this latest war-fed drought crisis, to buy a soft elephant of her own, perhaps called Nelly (only Nelly in African), with the money Uncle Peter was sending.

Unknown to the old lady gazing at the picture in her head, which she seemed to see better by gazing out through the window at the night sky's big screen, things hadn't in actuality worked like that. Amma's mother had got hold of a battery elephant. It was broken, medium-sized, torn and dirty-brown, and stained with only the God Poorly Boy prayed to knows what. A weeping woman whose child had just starved to death was, if not pleased, then willing to let it go when she saw Amma. And right now that same elephant was in turn being wept over and hair-rent by Amma's mother – the lifeless Amma and it clutched rib-cavingly close.

The broken elephant would continue its mission, going to comfort some other child – for a while. Though the old lady didn't know this was going on, she suspected as much. Irrationally, she felt her granddaughter would know for certain.

Something else of Poorly Boy's came to her – words said matter-of-factly.

"I had another Mummy once, you know, Mrs Lady. She gave me my job to do down here – the work the team 'n' me do, which keeps us out of bovver while we're waiting for Pat to come 'n' fetch us to go and help her. (It might not be for a long time 'cos Little Sheeps in't good enough by miles.) Someday she'll be so busy helping soft toys 'n' fings in heaven that she's going to need help real bad. She just won't be able to manage it on her own 'cos there ain't no spare angels these days like there used to be."

Poorly Boy suddenly awoke after falling asleep over prayers. He tilted the bedside lampshade to throw more light on Nelly and Crumble Bee, still embracing away the evils of the world. He stared curiously at Nelly – a look on his gaping mouth, open face and wide eyes of sheer wonder.

"You'll never guess who our Pat's got with her up there, and you'll never guess who the one who's with our Pat up there has given her battery elephant (with no batteries) to down here. I don't know the little black boy's name either."

Nelly looked puzzled, as she often did around Poorly Boy, regardless of Crumble Bee's warmth and silent, supportive stinkiness. Handsome he was – not in the usual sense, maybe, but in that strong, dark, bee kind of way some broken-dangly, purple-dye-runned bees have, which always sends lady elephants' hearts into flutters of pink elephantess-ness.

The Bad Badger

Poorly Boy was quite sick of Baby Kenneth. It was now some time since dinner and still – before, during and after – he was thumping around acting the Badger.

His father, Daddy Springy, could do nothing. He was at his wits' end, let alone the end of his carrot, with his son. Baby Kenneth was two and a half, and rabbits are even more terrifying than boys and girls at that age. Little Sheeps had tried fooling Kenneth into thinking he, Little Sheeps, was really Captain Vincent Aphid in disguise, and that the Captain wanted a truce.

"I don't want no juice!" growled Kenneth's tiny voice. "I am the Bad Badger of Bermundley and I don't take juice from no one. I go get my own."

They could have left him to do just that, only he wouldn't leave Poorly Boy, Little Sheeps and the team. He followed them everywhere, making a thorough nuisance of himself. This was especially upsetting as a new bench was going to be fitted in the Garden Shed Collectum later that afternoon and the team wanted to get the sick steering wheel well enough to steer the blue plastic Ford – rather out of focus and off colour without its walking aid of a pair of red pliers from a toy toolbox. This could only be achieved by a delicate procedure known as 'glue-splodging', which was still in its infancy. So much of a baby was it that Sue was sick, also that day, of telling it in its disguise of Poorly Boy not to be such a baby because two bowls of flour-and-water glue hadn't made the steering wheel any better yet.

"You've just got to wait until Dad and Uncle Peter get here, and you know they'll stick it on with proper plastic cement – but not you."

"I dun't want sticking!" growled Poorly Boy.

"I didn't mean that and you know it, you awkward little –"

"Rabbit!" growled Poorly Boy, pointing at Kenneth in one hand with the flour-and-water covered pliers in the other.

"Rabbit! Little rabbit! Baby Kenneth – he's the one who's awkward, not I!"

And that's how the day had bumped along with ailing steering to its twenty-four hour drive. But the afternoon was still young at half a turn to its 3 p.m. and the Bad Badger of Bermondsey (not 'Bermundley', as Kenneth said it) was still unvanquished. When Ben and Uncle Peter arrived with Ben's new tool bench for the Garden Shed Collectum, which he wished to take over from Poorly Boy's old toys by using a bribe, the 'Third World War' was over and the fourth, fifth and sixth were becoming history.

"Wow, it's a great bench, Dad! Fanks for letting me have the top for a top to have!"

"No problem, Poorly Boy! It's the sensible thing to do. Only you and Tiny so far have collected enough toys in the Garden Shed Collectum to give to poor children. Seeing as we've taken them to Oxfam, and most of the time the new shed's empty, I may as well use it."

Uncle Peter examined the sticky labels and lovely new woody bench smells.

"That's it," he said. "You'd never leave the old Garden Shed Infirmary for here, so Dad's giving his tools and lawnmower a new house to live in away from Sue's feet and the conservatory's rust – and you get a fine new bench top. Just feel its smoothness, Ben."

It was then they noticed Baby Kenneth was not bouncing happily over said bench top, but he was forcing Poorly Boy's hand to smear his (Baby Kenneth's) flour-gluey bottom across it. Ben's control was superb. Even the dent to his lorry a lady parking had given it that morning didn't collide with the Bad Badger.

"What's with your rabbit Pee Bee?" was all he said, though Uncle Peter was animated enough to take Sue's wash leather off its hook and start wiping.

"Don't Uncle Peter – and shush Dad, you'll upset him if you call him a rabbit, 'cos he ain't. He's the Bad Badger of Bermondsey."

(Baby Kenneth screamed, "Bermundley!" but only Poorly Boy heard it.)

"You mean him from the Commander Aphid comic?"

"Vincent Aphid, Dad," corrected Poorly Boy.

"I thought Baby Kenneth was leader of the Space Cadets," offered Uncle Peter.

"He ain't since you, Uncle Peter, took up wiv Geraldine from the office and dun't have time to read to him any more about stars, planets and canals going up Uranus."

"Mars," corrected Ben. "Going up Mars – or so it looks as we look at it from down here. It's optically presented to our sight as a flat disc."

Even the Bad Badger was looking at Ben in impressed silence.

"Be that as it may," scowled Uncle Peter, "but your wife and my sister is approaching, and knowing her as thoroughly as I do, I would say from her body language, through the open door here, that someone's in for some language strong enough to make them wish they were, right now, on a tranquil Martian canal."

Scared as they were, all three – Badger included – were impressed by Uncle Peter's expressive language.

The storm broke upon a rocky bench.

"What are you doing, Peter, with my wash leather?"

"Wiping Baby Kenneth's face, Mum," said Poorly Boy, beaming from invention to invention.

"Oh, its Baby Kenneth now, is it? Where's the Mad Beaver of Burnley got to?" she howled.

As one, all three politely corrected her.

"Whatever!" snarled Sue, making towards the Beaver – whatever, rabbit! – as if she was a vengeful Vincent Aphid.

"Oh, Mum, please don't hurt him!" whined Poorly Boy, doing his best Dickensian-urchin impression. "He's only two and he's having a bad time with it."

"*He's* having a bad time! What about me, with you, him and Whatever Beaver all day driving me to distraction!"

('Destruction,' thought the team, to be more exact, as one by one, by means of Poorly Boy's hands rushing from one shed to the other, they joined Baby Kenneth on the new bench. They only thought it – not daring to speak to Sue's bodily language.)

Uncle Peter and Ben also remained silent onlookers of the seventh world conflagration now in progress. Ben, though, was expecting at any moment the day to steer into a 'Your Son Day' cul-de-sac and park on him. 'Your Son Days' occurred whenever Sue disowned any twenty-four hour period or part of it; she would blame it on Ben's fathering Poorly Boy – alone – at some time or other five years and nine months previously, when she was presumably an innocent bystander. Bad boys are always brought into the world by their fathers.

As Ben was expecting, Sue did give birth to a particularly bouncing, "Your Son has terrorised me today with silly demands for bowls of flour glue whilst Baby Kenneth has been a thoroughly naughty bear, before, during and after lunch. What are you doing with my wash leather Peter?"

Uncle Peter's mouth gaped open wide enough for his sister to stuff the wash leather inside. She didn't, but neither did he get chance to reply.

"Mummy, Mummy," said young Shakespeare, "it's all been a misunderstandable. You know how Commander Aphid is pitying his whites against his swearing enemy, that nasty London Badger? And you know how the good guys – the cellulite Planktons – have been wiped out by 'the rodent who is no gent', as Commander Aphid calls him?"

Sue glared at Ben.

"Are beavers rodents?" she asked.

"Badgers," Ben replied. "They are if Commander Vincent T Aphid says so," settled Poorly Boy definitively. Uncle Peter opened his mouth again but Poorly Boy anticipated:

"Tony".

Sue broke this contemplative mood with another verbal wash leather.

"What has any of this to do with either Kenneth or Poorly Boy's inexcusable behaviour?"

"Poorly Boy had a go at wash-leathering in turn.

"Look, Mummy – if Uncle Peter hadn't decided to be in love with Geraldine every night, then Baby Kenneth wouldn't be going mad about my comics. It's all he's got to listen to now after tea when you 'n' dad read them to the team and me. You know how interested he is in outer space. He was even leader of the Space Cadets, with Nocky and Baby Kenneth's plastic Christmas-cracker rabbit, Jimmy, as Invaders of Naughty Planets and Little Sheeps and Nelly as Bandagers of Mr Crumble Bee the Space Bee Monster's monstrous danglies? Well you can't blame a poor little inquisitive rabbit if he gets carried away wiv Bad Badgers, can you? And as for me, all I wanted to do was mend my Ford's broken steering wheel – which in't wrong at all, is it, Dad?"

Ben was thinking over Uncle Peter being in love with Geraldine every night and was caught unawares by this most difficult wash leather Poorly Boy had got him into – one which could see him getting into a verbal bucketful of them from all three unless he was very tactful. As usual, he'd seen the way Poorly Boy was using his, and he was about to help him wipe things up.

"Of course wanting to mend your toys isn't wrong, Pee Bee. Why, with me on the lorries so much and Peter now seeing as much of Geraldine as he is ..." (During the pause, Sue caught Ben's sly look at Uncle Peter.) "It's just a pity Mum is the homely sort – not very mechanical and more into ordinary household matters."

Poorly Boy pouted at Sue, and Ben smiled at her in a patronisingly sympathetic way, as you would to a small child who knew no better and wasn't meant to.

"I did mix the silly glue up for him, didn't I?" she said defensively.

"But you didn't tell him it was the wrong sort, did you?" accused Ben.

"I did so, but he wouldn't listen!" defended the defendant.

Uncle Peter decided to settle out of court – however reluctantly.

"Look Poorly Boy – bring Baby Kenneth round and I'll read my astronomical books to him, sat on my knee like I used to."

"What about Geraldine?" Ben couldn't help himself.

"What concern is it of yours?" Sue couldn't help herself.

"She can help Uncle Peter read to us, Mum," settled Poorly Boy brightly. "She's good at stuff like that, in't she, Uncle Peter? That's why she's lately been doing her cold school work round at your house, where it's warmer. She'd much rather have me and Kenneth there than just her and you 'cos it'd be lots more fun and warmer wiv five of us, counting your Floppy Duck."

Baby Kenneth leapt over from the bench and snuggled in Poorly Boy's and Uncle Peter's hands.

"Er, Geraldine will be there sweetheart, but it's her Open University Course she's been doing, and I've been helping her, yes."

"That's what I mean, Uncle Peter. Kenneth and me can help her *close* it. You don't want open schools in winter – and *that's* the big school you go to on a laptop, and carrying hers in could be slippery. She might fall and hurt herself if the doors open this winter and it's icy on the carpets and you're all alone wiv her. Don't worry no more. Me 'n' Baby Kenneth will sort you out."

Baby Kenneth still held Uncle Peter's hand as the shed door was closed behind them all. Ben's head was down, but from the side the ends of his grin could be seen as mouth touched ear. As they walked back to the house, Uncle Peter was glaring at Ben from the right and Sue from the left. Sue's glare was about Geraldine, as Uncle Peter's was. Poorly Boy was chittering on happily. Uncle Peter's attention was drawn to it by Baby Kenneth's tugging at his sleeve.

"You ain't listening, Uncle Peter and Dad. Baby Kenneth's got a good idea. He says we can keep tins and jars and empty boxes of Poppo Flakes wiv money in on top of the bench to give to poor children. Money's easier to get than toys, so if we get too much for the bench we can take your tools back out, Dad, to make more room for Poppo Flakes and coffee jars to put it in. We can start it right now after tea, seeing as you're all here to give something, and we can get money off Geraldine later at your house. Mum can't give nuffink because she's got to buy ordinary, homely things for the house."

Sue was grinning like an expensive new wash leather.

Arthur and the X-Ray Machine

Had you been five years old and wanting to chop a big toe off your own foot, then the latest equipment in the Garden Shed Infirmary would have been ideal. Like all X-ray machines, if misused, it would have been dangerous.

It was thanks to Little Sheeps that this device for health and healing was presently easing the workload for staff and Poorly Boy alike – not because it was switched on and working (in fact, it didn't have a switch), but because it was standing there doing nothing. It was what Little Sheeps called the 'Mirror Model X-ray Machine'. Nelly called it the 'Plain Daft Smashed Mirror', because, to be accurate, that's what it was.

It had started life as Ben's shaving mirror, becoming, when it was older, Poorly Boy's latest addition to the onion bench after he'd begged it when Sue bought Ben a new mirror with a less flimsy support stand. Poorly Boy usually got whatever he pleaded for, and Ben reluctantly, and against Sue's passionate counter-pleading, had seriously warned Poorly Boy about touching it once Ben had fixed it firmly to a strong wooden grooved plinth containing the frame near the onions on Poorly Boy's bench.

Ben, however, hadn't told Little Sheeps not to touch it; and as the woolly one had plans for an X-ray machine which just happened to be based on a shaving mirror, all he needed to do was put a large crack in it with a piece of glass jaggedly removed. Ideally the crack would be about a child's-toe width at the top, tapering to a mere few millimetres at the bottom. Such a mirror-length crack could be obtained, Little Sheeps felt, by standing Poorly Boy on tiptoes, raising Poorly Boy's arms and using Poorly Boy's hands to dislodge the mirror till it fell off the onion bench onto the Garden Shed Infirmary floor, narrowly missing Poorly Boy's big toe. That way, hopefully, the ideal crack for the job would be secured, though this was hardly the kind of security Ben had envisaged for his shaving mirror's future.

To Little Sheep's delight – and of course Poorly Boy's – the crack was perfect from top to bottom. Unfortunately the plastic frame was broken right through, as they found after installing it back on the bench on its new gliding, state-of-the-art onion base for quick and easy movement to anywhere in the Garden Shed Infirmary – or Poorly Boy's foot. X-ray equipment might be needed to draw blood.

"You ain't using my machine properly, Poorly Boy." Little Sheeps was irritated by Poorly Boy abusing his brainchild. "It's not really designed for flexing arm muscles in front of while our patients are kept waiting for important X-rays and no work's getting done."

"Oh, do shut up bleating, Little Sheeps." Poorly Boy was irritated too. "It was you who said I should do some training before lifting heavy weights. All I'm doing is making sure my arm muscles are standing up and ready for hard work!"

"It's also a great X-ray of two halves of a Poorly Boy," observed Nelly whilst being flexed in Poorly Boy's left X-ray plate, split into two by a mirror with a dirty great crack up its middle.

The missing piece of wedge-shaped glass was lying on the floor, waiting for Poorly Boy to cut himself – again – or else a poor team member or patient or Nelly! Nelly was not impressed by Little Sheep's technological innovations in general, none of which she felt were boons to health. This one in particular had already claimed a small wound on one of the fingers smearing blood on her right now.

"In any case," she went on, while Poorly Boy continued to flex and pump ever so small amounts of blood from his outstretched finger on to her pink trunk, "you don't even get to see inside of anything – only two halves and a dirty big crack."

"Yes, but it's the 'crack', as you call it, which is the X-ray part itself," pointed out the arm-tiring Poorly Boy. "You're not supposed to see anything inside with this particular model – are you, Little Sheeps? – because it's more advanced than the simple sort of X-ray thingies you find in people hospitals."

Nelly abruptly made Poorly Boy stop blood-pumping.

"Then what use is it?" She glared into the mirror from above her blood-stained trunk.

Little Sheeps sighed exasperatedly.

"This is so powerful that you get to see right through things," he said proudly. By way of clarification, he continued in the manner used by all knowledgeable sheep to lecture young pink elephants: "'Tain't no use seeing inside things with equipment now in use everywhere, 'cos with that plug-into-the-wall type all you get is very low power; the insides of the objects spoil the view so you can't see right through them to the back of the equipment, which is what you really wanted. Blood, guts, breath, bones, stitches and stuffing – all yucky stuff – gets in the way. This one – this one", he repeated for extra effect, "is onion-pong-powered. And onion-powered pongs are the pongiest, most powerful source of pong power unknown to man in the whole universal, but not …"

Poorly Boy bowed low with raised-arm-to-floor flourish, to salute the esteemed inventor, who repeated for effect:

"But not to Little Sheeps."

As Little Sheeps finished his speech, Poorly Boy stood up from his elaborate bow, his face deadpan serious as if defying everybody else's not to be.

Nelly, exasperated, sat the exhausted arm flexor in a heap with her on the woodchip floor. Little Sheeps peered down at them from his elevated position of genius of the onion bench, next to his latest masterpiece.

"Are you ready to get with the morning's important job, or do we go on wasting time with ignoramusphants like Nelly till dinner?"

Nelly had lost too much blood to be bothered any more. Poorly Boy stuck out his tongue as always when determined, sat Nelly lovingly and gently on the floor and stood, one aching arm holding the other, helping it to flex.

"Right!" he exclaimed affirmatively. "Me 'n' the wheelbarrow/ambulance is off to do what has to be done to do it properly."

With such wise words headaching in the ears of each soft toy and onion in the Garden Shed Infirmary, Poorly Boy, all tiredness behind him, moved in jaw-jutting thrust of purpose door-wards. The ambulance majestically swept out into the garden like a one-wheeled red plastic ship with an oddly dismembered face decoration on its four sides, followed by a stiff breeze of Captain Blackbeard Poorly Boy at its two yellow tiller handles.

The Garden Shed Infirmary fell silent in deep thought and ponder. Nelly looked into Little Sheeps' cunning eyes, Daddy Springy's wise ones, Crumble Bee's stupid ones and Baby Kenneth's curious ones as, on his nose end and dangerously close, Baby Kenneth examined the wickedly sharp triangular glass shard Little Sheeps had discarded while making X-rays possible. Not one of the team spoke, though no doubt they were deeply worried for the welfare of, if not their master, then their dearest human friend – for they would never have allowed Poorly Boy to be master over them. Would he, they no doubt wondered, survive his mission with his own health only delicate at best, and little muscular power in his frail body? Most importantly of all, would he persuade Sue, with the cunning Little-Sheeps-and-Poorly-Boy-devised plan behind the mission, to let him keep the X-ray machine, though it could be dangerous in the wrong hands and paws? Nelly, with bleakly doubting eyes, doubted it.

Joan was surprised to hear Poorly Boy's cheerful:

"Hello, Joannie. Can we come in and save you, please? Mummy's with me and's given me permission!"

The day was warm and the window open, giving a good view of Sue's puzzled and embarrassed shrug.

The wheelbarrow/ambulance stayed outside guarding the entrance as Joan, the old lady who lived next door, happily took Poorly Boy and Sue into the lounge. This was where Poorly Boy – usually a small eater – usually crumbled his way through three chocolate digestives. Joan loved having young neighbours, and she felt extra warmth towards them as it was the second time she'd been with Sue that morning. Today's company made her feel especially fond of them on account of Poorly Boy's obvious concern for her.

Joan and Sue watched fascinated while Poorly Boy caught crumbs planning escape from his plate with his finger and gave his arm another flex to ensure the biscuits went to live in their muscles.

"Are you bodybuilding, Poorly Boy?" Joan chuckled.

Sue coughed uneasily and spoke to Joan, momentarily preoccupied crumb-hunting:

"He says he and the team have been waiting for the lorry to arrive, but Daddy Springy says they must have missed it during their argument over Little Sheeps' X-ray machine."

Joan, like most older-people, was quicker on the uptake than those years younger and replied, a couple of crumb-hunt captives later, that he must have somehow got confused while listening to her telling Sue about iron tablets.

"He must think I'm having a new path put down, or something really heavy, and the little treasure's come with his toy wheelbarrow and tiny muscles to lift and lay it for me! Oh, what a beautiful child he is!"

Poorly Boy gave up the last crumb when it ran into the carpet undergrowth beneath the table and escaped. Not to be beaten he chased after another biscuit with his hand inside the packet, rummaging for more tasty animal-fat life at the bottom.

"No, I ain't beautiful!" he spluttered indignantly, disdain dribbling full-mouthed, chocolate chin to T- shirt. "I didn't want you carrying iron tablets once the big men had delivered the massive box, that's all. They're really heavy, they are, and anyway me and the team aren't sure the Doctor's right when he tells you you're short of metal. You're very old to be swallowing that much iron. One thing is, it could rust wiv the water you drink; and another is, it means your Arthur's going to get worse too with the extra weight he's got to lift if you fall over."

Joan's long dead husband hadn't been called Arthur and she quickly realised that Poorly Boy must mean her arthritis.

Poorly Boy had no time to lose and a point to prove:

"Come on, then – let's go to Little Sheeps' machine before Mum throws it out. Stand clear, Joannie and Mum, while I carry the big box of iron tablets out to the wheelbarrow/ambulance. Let's go to the Garden Shed Infirmary. Where are you keeping such a huge package? It's not sticking out from anywhere. Have you left it round the side of the house 'cos it's too big to get through the door? Don't worry – I can split things into smaller chunks with my plastic saw. Lorry drivers are like my dad and in a hurry to do everything in a hurry. They hurry up and spoil everything, they do, Mum says, so they'll have cleared off and left you to it, like Dad does Mum."

Joan noticed, then withdrew her glance quickly, that Sue flushed red.

Poorly Boy was surprised and disappointed at the smallness of the box of tablets when Joan pointed it out on the table at which Poorly Boy was seated. They were near his plate and he'd been playing with the box while eating. His scowl lasted just long enough to brood over the fact that he'd be unable to show how strong he was to the two grown-ups and the team. The realisation blossomed that his slight concern over his poorly heart's weightlifting abilities wouldn't be tested after all; so at least he ought to still be alive when they reached the Garden Shed Infirmary to show off Little Sheeps' technological brain lamb.

He was still insistent that he carry the tablets outside to place them in the wheelbarrow/ambulance. Sue protested and warned him not to fall with them, while he protested back that if she'd really been a good caring mother, she'd be more worried about his poorly heart falling over than the silly box's heart getting squished. Joan meanwhile strolled behind this carnival, an amused smile on her lined but well-entertained face.

At the ever half-open door to the Garden Shed infirmary, Poorly Boy stopped arguing and turned to face his mother, his arms raised, hands open as if stilling chattering hordes before an important speech.

"Now, Mum, don't go on at Little Sheeps when you see his invention, 'cos you won't like it. You'll say it's dangerous and that it's got to go. Just be careful that when you yell at him you do it softly as he's sheepish and easily hurt. His ears are bad and his legs easily break." He stopped and pushed his right palm against the air, testing to make sure it was still holding Sue fast behind it. "I dun't mind you chucking it out, but only if you promise before you go in to let Little Sheeps do what he has to do with it before it goes out."

She opened her mouth to yell at Poorly boy, as any mother would in a situation like this, but the air rushed in to prevent her – or rather, Joan's light and spry unconcerned:

"Of course we don't mind Little Sheeps using his dangerous machine, do we, Sue? We trust him and you, sweetheart. We know you're only doing the best for my tablets and me. Promise there's no electricals involved though, won't you?" she added as the sole cautionary note.

Poorly Boy withdrew his arms and rushed inside accompanied by the air.

Naturally, Sue spluttered when she saw Ben's shaving mirror, and with the same splutter she learnt by following Joan's pointed finger towards Poorly Boy and the onion bench that this indeed was the home of the unique and sensitive machine. Joan's eyes were as big as the plaques on her living-room walls, and Sue looked in need of a chair to either sit on or brain her only child with.

"Now watch," announced the only child. "Joan," – Poorly Boy looked up at the lady, his eyes bigger and more charming than any wall plate or sun smiling an April shower away – "may I please pass an iron pill to Little Sheeps for X-ray?"

Joan nodded an eager affirmative, and Poorly Boy broke the seal and carried regally a tiny white capsule outstretched towards Little Sheeps (the palm of the hand with the pill being supported underneath by the other hand as if it weighed a steel town full of foundries).

He explained what was going on.

"You see, Little Sheeps tells me to hold the iron up in front of the machine's screen – or broke mirror for those who dun't understand such things as this – but there is nothing to be seen. The tablet becomes invisible in the middle of the bit where the glass is missing." Poorly Boy's brows were drawn low. They met in the middle, giving him a severe look. "That isn't because the tablet is too small to be shown back, because there's a whacking great piece of glass missing out of the middle, so don't say it is!"

None did.

"It is because there is very little iron in these tablets the doctor has given Joannie to take." He turned to the women, like a professor towards his class. "The machine is set to X-ray for an iron present in the tablet's tummy, and it has found not even enough to show a little picture of. Therefore if Joannie was to swallow the whole lot at once, her Arthur wouldn't have to worry none about her ever moving again because she was too heavy. He wouldn't need a crane or wheels fitted to her or to margarine the floor to slide her on neither. In't Little Sheeps clever?"

Even one as young as Baby Kenneth looked up at Poorly Boy as if his explanation of a difficult procedure was good enough for baby rabbits, and thus fully grown women. Poorly Boy frowned even deeper in the silence following Little Sheeps' demonstration. Surely Baby Kenneth had been on his nose when he'd last seen him! Nobody there had noticed or moved him. And that piece of glass X-ray machine Little Sheeps had thrown on the floor unwanted – that piece looking very sharp and nasty – wasn't it closer to Baby Kenneth's nose when he last saw it, not near the onion bench, glinting at him from the top of the full rubbish bin? It must have been the breeze or Arthur that warned Baby Kenneth to stay away from sharp edges and blew (or put) the glinty bit out of harm's way.

"Come on!" said Sue, breaking Poorly Boy's train of thought. It was then he also caught sight of what appeared to be a blue plastic handle propped just the other side of the bin by the onion bench.

"Now we know it's safe for Joan to take such small amounts of iron, we'd better go and have a cup of tea. It's about time for her dose." There was a curious sort of laughter tone in Sue's voice which made Poorly Boy look at her suspiciously. She smiled a perfectly innocent smile, gleaming at him. "Oh, there it is. Pass me my blue dustpan propped by the onion bench, will you, Poorly Boy? Arthur must have left it behind after we heard a crash of glass earlier this morning and he peered round the Garden Shed Infirmary door and saw you all working hard. He came and told me everything was all right, though – no harm done – and it was only Little Sheeps constructing a strange machine. May I try it before I get rid of it, Poorly Boy – see if it can see right through me like I can you?"

But Poorly Boy didn't really hear. He was too angry with Arthur. What a sneak! No wonder he kept out the way and you never caught sight of him creeping around, causing trouble and spoiling plans!

Alice

It wasn't good. Crouched too long studying, he became aware of the pain in his right hip. Poorly Boy sighed, tried to stand and fell over backwards, hitting his head on the garden path. Obvious, though it was, that he was unconscious, bleeding from a gash above his ear and maybe in a coma, there was nothing he could do other than run to the Garden Shed Infirmary for emergency treatment.

"Give me all the details." Nelly urgently tended the injured baby rabbit.

"Me 'n' Baby Kenneth were looking at the broken wheel on the wheelbarrow/ambulance and I crouched down holding Baby Kenneth, so's he could see better where the axle had gone wobbly. I got cramp and fell over, as I lost balance standing, and Baby Kenneth banged his poor head badly. "Will he live, Nelly, and be our beloved bunny again and not have headaches or be in a comma all his life?"

"Oh, don't cry, Poorly Boy!" reassured Little Sheeps. "Won't be long before baby bunny'll be chucking lettuce in the air, giggling buckets and sticking carrots in Nelly's trunk in the morning, just like he always does!"

Nelly glared at the woolly would-be comedian – a glare of such contempt for one who could say such cold, heartless things at a time of national emergency.

"If you can't be serious, be gone!" she commanded, eyes boring into Little Sheeps' crafty ones, which turned away like the eyes of a naughty child. "Go with Poorly Boy and look after him. You can see how upset he is. I want him away from here while Mr Crumble Bee examines Baby Kenneth."

Outside the Garden Shed Infirmary as the sunny garden sang birdsongs, Poorly Boy didn't appear too upset to Little Sheeps.

"Stop dancing about the flower beds, trying to see how close to the snapdragons you can get before they snap at your legs – which means how close you get before you just happen to knock off a head so's you can play opening its mouth between your fingers without actually picking a head off, just in case Mum sees you and tells you off. S'not fair 'cos Nelly got on to me that you was upset by what I said – and you aren't in the least, so I got a telling off for nothing! You got me sent out of the Garden Shed Infirmary just when things were getting' interesting. Crumble Bee was bound to say something daft and probably open Kenneth's stomach up to get to the cut on his head!"

"All right then," said Poorly Boy, playing with a snapdragon head. "Tell you what: let's go get rabbit blood from the kitchen and rush back in time for the best bit when Crumble Bee opens Kenneth up."

"Not the whole jar you're not – that's best supermarket organic!" Sue was firm. "Get your dirty fingers out and stop feeding jam to the snapdragon. If you want some of it you can have a sandwich."

"Great, Mum!" replied Poorly Boy. "I'll just go and stick Snappy back on his stalk while you make Baby Kenneth's four slices. Then me 'n' Little Sheeps will take them to him so's he can have his dinner before Mr Crumble Bee cuts him up."

After some argument, it was decided that two slices would be enough for a rabbit about to undergo surgery, and on the way to the Garden Shed infirmary Poorly Boy decided it would be safer to have the sandwiches himself.

"Don't want to have Baby Kenneth in two halves only to find chunks of bread in Mr Crumble Bee's way getting from rabbit stomach to brain!" Poorly Boy finished munching and looked down at the sheep in one hand and the jammy fingers on the other. "OK – so much, so fast."

"Don't you mean 'so far, so good'?" queried Little Sheeps, to whom Poorly Boy gave the look of a disgusted Poorly Boy being very disgusted indeed.

"Just do as I do for once, and don't be such a pig in the bottom, pulling me out over everythin' I say!"

"Up," said Little Sheeps quietly, unable to help himself: "pulling me up."

It was then that Poorly Boy smeared jam on Little Sheeps' paws, and he understandably thought Poorly Boy must be angry with him, which though true wasn't the reason for it.

"What I want you to do, sheepy mate of mine, is try to stick Snappy's head on (I've had a go, so Mum thinks), and then we can both say this jam's the wrong stickability for sticking heads on, see?"

"Where's Woolly Bully?" snapped Nelly when a jammy-faced Poorly Boy re-entered the Garden Shed Infirmary.

"He's covered in jam, playing in the flower beds. Flipped at last, I fink he has."

Nelly nodded at Poorly Boy, one of those it-was-bound-to-happen-sooner-or-later-type nods.

"As you see," – she changed the subject – "Mr Crumble Bee has done a serious operation and stuck a plaster near Baby Kenneth's ear where he pulled a lump of garden path out of Baby Kenneth's brain. If he hadn't been successful, Baby Kenneth would have been in a full stop for the rest of his life."

"Comma, you mean," corrected Poorly Boy.

"Crumble Bee's a soft-toy surgeon, not a professor of English. 'Coma, you both mean," explained Daddy Springy, who was on the onion bench in the plastic microwave dish operating table/tray, holding his young son's paw as Baby Kenneth recovered from his ordeal. "A coma is a long state of unconsciousness," he went on.

"Yes, like Little Sheeps ever since we've known him, and most likely for the rest of his bleating life!" said Nelly with little charity.

Poorly Boy felt guilty suddenly. He thought that his dear friend was in need of defending.

"Actually Little Sheeps is fixing a snapdragon's head on, and I've got Baby Kenneth's blood transfusion all over my lips, sweatshirt, hair, ears and trouser behind."

"Good!" said Nelly firmly. "You're a good boy, Poorly Boy. Timed perfectly! It's well known that young rabbits need the right type of jam to replace what they lose during surgery exactly ten minutes to two hours after being stitched up. Stitches leak a lot, you see. The only trouble is, you've the wrong sort on your face and bum. It's blackcurrant home-made two-and-a-half-year-olds need not shop organic strawberry, until they're their dad's age."

"Oh, in't that funny, Nelly? Little Sheeps 'n' me found the snapdragon head won't go back on with the thin Lippo's supermarket stuff. 'Taint much good for greasin' axles either."

Though Sue had learnt to like Mr Brown, she didn't find the old gentleman easy to get on with. He lived opposite. His wife and family had left long ago on account of his temper and increasingly silent ways of keeping himself to himself. Sue's friendship with him was continually on and off, and right now it was definitely off over some odd disagreement. Duncan Brown's only constant friend was Poorly Boy, whose friendship with the whole world, if it would let him, would be for life.

However, this particular month was one in which Duncan needed Sue as well as Poorly Boy, and it was very unfortunate that it should be an off month for friendship with the lad's mother. Duncan was a great grower of things, as Poorly Boy reminded Sue.

"Mr Brown has fruit bushes, Mum, and, now I've explained why you've got to have the right stuff for the job, I know you'll come and help me carry a few jars."

Duncan sat with the curtains half drawn. He was reading the letter once more to make sure of the time they'd come for him two days from now. He wasn't sad – he was too tired – but he hoped Poorly Boy would manage to bring Sue and that their hurriedly cobbled-together plan would work. He heard voices, and one tall and one small form passed the window and rang the doorbell. A little later the bell rang again and Duncan closed the suitcase in his bedroom, where he was packing, and went downstairs to let his young friend in.

"It's not been out of the oven long, Mr Brown – just enough for Mum to let me not burn Little Sheeps' paws bringing it to you. It's your favourite – cottage pie. Seeing as you're going where there's lots of spices, Mum's put plenty of pepper on, just as you like it! Mum was crying, Mr Brown, but I told her not to. I told her you'll be happy in a place where the name of it says there's plenty of hot spices, because you love making jam and cooking meals. Mum knew Mrs Brown, but I never met her."

As the three of them, including Little Sheeps, tucked in to cottage pie they looked back on the drama they'd cooked up to get Sue friends with Duncan. Then the three shed some tears.

"I'm going to miss you, precious," said Duncan tenderly.

"Me 'n' the team will miss you more than you'll miss us. We love you, Mr Brown – even though you and us know you make 'orrible jam!"

They giggled before crying again.

"Don't know how you expect me to manage fixing flower heads on until you come home, Mr Brown!" Poorly Boy was trying to be cheerful.

"I'm pleased your mum will bring you all to the hospice, Poorly Boy," said Duncan after the handkerchief had gone the rounds and Little Sheeps had handed it back.

The old man said drily that they could bring him a jar of shop-bought jam. Poorly Boy asked if he might have the handkerchief once more, after which he returned it. The three fell silent staring at the snapdragon's head, which Poorly Boy had taken out of his pocket and placed on the table as a present for Duncan.

"I'm going to wash the blood off and press it in a thick book, as we've done with other flowers, so Snappy will live for ever."

No sooner had Mr Brown said it than the phrase 'for ever' echoed and boomed loudly through his head. He swallowed noticeably enough for Poorly Boy to be concerned that his throat had stuck.

That evening, Poorly Boy and the team were watching through the ever half-open doorway of the Garden Shed Infirmary. The shadows of hedges, fences and flowers were playing hide and seek with one another. Poorly Boy ended his tale of how the day's concerns had worked out, and they all continued to watch for the moment they loved most: when the fence shadow grew big enough to creep up and catch the bush shadow trying to hide beside the Garden Shed Infirmary.

Nobody was speaking, so Nelly did, as if talking to the shadows.

"I know why the phrase 'for ever' hurt Mr Brown. It's got a sharp jagged letter at the beginning and an even sharper one halfway along so people get 'for ever' stuck in their throats when saying it. Elephants can use it without it cutting, because of our elastic trunks. Maybe that's another reason why elephants live longer than people – 'for ever' doesn't cause us pain."

Duncan unpacked the suitcase. Before going downstairs for his first evening meal at the boarding house close by the hospice where Alice was, he polished his gold ring (as he made a point of doing) on the shirt tails he always wore outside his trousers. Usually he'd nowhere to go, so informality allowed his shirts and vests full freedom. On this night he dressed formally smart. He'd been to see a lady. He polished his ring on his tie, and this time he raised the hand and kissed the finger.

Comparative Fish Shops

"You aren't."

"I am."

"You can't."

"I can."

"That's daft."

"It's not."

"Is too."

"Oh, rot!"

They were looking more fish hooks than daggers into each other's eyes. So close were they together that their stares went curvily deep enough to see inside each other's socks. It was Little Sheeps who started to chuckle first; only a moment later, Poorly Boy followed.

"Aw, Little Sheeps, we're talking in poetry!"

Poorly Boy rolled on his back, cycling his legs in the air. They were in the Garden Shed Infirmary, discussing something really too serious for hilarity, though it needed Nelly to point this out to them.

"Stop giggling, idiots, and be serious. Look at the possible constipations of what you're saying, Poorly Boy."

"I feel you mean 'consequences', Nelly." Little Sheeps looked very serious as he said it, his uncanny sense of what's right and what's not in the use of the English language having curtailed his merriment.

Nelly ignored his eloquence and went on with her own: "You can't go about stealing people's supper and trying to bring it back to life – even if you do leave the chips behind because they go soggy and die in water. It's not good to make those you love go hungry."

Little Sheeps nodded agreement as he sat in Poorly Boy's hand.

"She's right, son: fish 'n' chips once a week on a Friday night, and you'd pinch the very batter out of their mouths – even if you do leave the sausage behind because you say fish and sausage don't get on in the same box together without fighting."

"Disguising, isn't it?" affirmed Nelly.

"Gusting," said Little Sheeps in his role of World's Leading Sheeply Custodian of the English Tongue.

"No such word as 'gusting'," replied Nelly as if speaking to a fleece-covered fool.

Little Sheeps decided this was getting hard, and let it go.

The plan involved Duncan, who was lonely and bored enough with his own company to agree to anything, no matter how stupid. As long as it meant someone to do it with such as Poorly Boy, who was the only one who did anything with him, he'd gladly aid any madcap schemes. In fact, he'd even enter into the spirit of whatever nonsense Poorly Boy wanted him to participate in.

But as he sat in his rundown red car, with the sky threatening with grey fists to get even with him for helping to poach a family's supper, he wondered if it might be better to try talking Poorly Boy out of it when the lad arrived carrying the spoils.

He was so sat, scowlingly pondering the steering wheel, wishing for decisiveness, when a tiny fist rapped on the side window. This fist belonged to Poorly Boy and not the sky. Duncan leant across and unlocked the door – a thing he'd not done earlier in case Ben and Poorly Boy's Uncle Peter came out, and not his co-conspirator.

"Here, Mr Brown – take the fishes off of me," said Poorly Boy, all urgent whispers and tongue-biting haste. "Ow!" he exclaimed, sulkily sitting down beside Duncan, who, though still scowlingly contemplating the steering wheel for ideas of what he was going to say to discourage the boy from his fish-brained scheme, now sat with a transparent sandwich box on his lap. The loose lid started to slip, and both boy and old man banged heads retrieving it. Duncan was about to replace the lid when he saw what was in the box: one lonely chip (which uncomfortably reminded Duncan of himself) shared the box with Ben's fried haddock, Uncle Peter's cod and Sue's battered sausage. Poorly Boy, rubbing his head and trying to see his tongue in the rear-view mirror by standing and sticking it out, caught Duncan staring box-wards.

"Mum's sausage, that is, Mr Brown. It got in by mistake, so we'll take it back after we've done our plan."

"*Your* plan," corrected Mr Brown.

"Mine and Little Sheeps'," said Poorly Boy, fishing the sheep out of his Puffa-jacket pocket and perching him on the dashboard, looking in at them. Poorly Boy settled down, waiting, looking satisfied with himself. After a minute he looked questioningly up at Duncan: "Why aren't we moving, Mr Brown?" he enquired indignantly. "If we don't get off, they'll know something's wrong when Mum opens the oven where she puts the fishes after Dad brought them in from the chippy."

"Do you think this is such a good idea, Poorly Boy?"

The steering wheel had at last been decisive.

"Little Sheeps does – and that's good enough for you and me."

Poorly Boy's reply sounded decisive to Duncan, so he did as Little Sheeps wished and drove off.

Sue was about to open the oven door as the car drove away and headed for the river. She had one of her feelings just as her hand grasped the handle. Straightening, she turned and looked at Nelly on the kitchen table. What was Nelly trying to tell her? Anything? Or was it nothing more than Sue's own tiredness? Some days were very long with Poorly Boy, and this had been an especially difficult week – one fraught with concern over the real reason why he was doing such odd things. It was then Sue saw Nelly was pointing with her bottom at a piece of notepaper underneath her.

"Mr Brown, what are sausages made of?"

"Pork, Poorly Boy. Why?"

They were driving to the river; the sky, noted Duncan, was still shaking fists menacingly slowly, only darker ones than before.

"If I eat sausages – which I love – I eat pork, and pork is pigs – that's right?"

"Yes, Poorly Boy."

The lad was nodding slowly. He reached forward and took Little Sheeps to cuddle.

"I like fish paste, fishcakes and fish fingers, but I won't eat proper fish – only sometimes from another fish shop."

That last mysteriously puzzling remark Duncan ignored for the moment.

"What's 'proper fish', Poorly Boy?"

"In a way, it's this in the box, because it looks as if it can be made to swim again. It's fish-shaped, so it's a bit proper – only not proper because it's not cooked proper from where it's cooked from. But it is the first way proper, so it should swim, still being fish shaped, if it's put in a river, even if it dun't taste nice. Dad gives me the fish off his fishing line to put back in, which means they can live out of water."

There were a few spots of fist on the windscreen.

"But it's not so with these," Poorly Boy sighed, looking round at the box on the back seat.

"You told me something of that yesterday, Poorly Boy, when Little Sheeps and you came across with your plan – also about your Mum being upset with you for trying to re-fly dead butterflies, ladybirds and things. She'd found you dropping an oven-ready chicken out of the bedroom window. Why Poorly Boy? Why try making dead things live?"

Poorly Boy, businesslike-rapid, replaced Little Sheeps on the dashboard. He placed his hands together between his thighs.

"Because you've got to try, Mr Brown, even if it's only once in a lifetime. Headless chickens without feathers, insects without wings – try just once when you're growing up; and if you're me you go on trying for ever. Try everything to make it better, even further than the point where all hope's gone and died. A little girl wiv a pet hamster she loved and cared for has it go still one night, and the light's leave its eyes that shone pictures of the girl's smile. What does she do? She tries to put it on its feet, but it can't stand cos the light's gone for ever.

That dun't stop her trying again when her rabbit's legs go and her budgie's wings fall down and her cat's miaow and her doggy's bark stop working."

Duncan wondered why the girl was so unfortunate with her pets, but he simply said, "I see, Poorly Boy."

"Don't you think you owe me an explanation too?" Little Sheeps, tired as he was, couldn't help feel proud that Nelly had used and pronounced the word correctly.

"We'd rather go to sleep and tell you tomorrow," he yawned, on the pillow beside Poorly Boy.

Nelly was not sleepy. She jumped out of Poorly Boy's hand from the bedside cabinet, landing on top of the sheep, who yelled and scurried under the bedclothes. Though Poorly Boy giggled, he stopped as Nelly threateningly poked her trunk at his nostril.

"I want to know now; and if you don't tell me – well, you've seen what this trunk can do and you'll never be too big not to have a nosebleed."

Poorly Boy sighed and sat up, propping himself rather uncomfortably on elbow and pillow – but not on Nelly, who he'd made sure he'd placed on the cabinet out of elbow's way. Little Sheeps was not so fortunate; he got the left one in his eye, but it didn't matter much as he wasn't the one doing the threatening. Poorly Boy smiled weakly. Little Sheeps now sat beside Nelly, rubbing his ear (which he said was also damaged for ever), his foot, knee and leg (which was broken yet again, so he claimed). Poorly Boy ignored the whingeing sheep and concentrated his smile on Nelly – the one with the trunk.

"You know, I know how to open the oven, like you know I know how to put chairs against windows, throw chickens out and open gates one-handed. I also know you can't write, and Mr Brown wrote that note under my bum you left so Mum knew where you were and what you done!" The trunk appeared no less dangerous.

"Yes, Nelly, but you don't know why."

"Oh, but I do. You put those fish in the river to see if they would swim off, headless and tailless, you idiot! Chickens out of windows! Fried fish in rivers! Even sausages – as if pigs swam! You're a mantis, Poorly Boy, you are!"

Little Sheeps was sulking, so he had no intention of giving Nelly a 'menace' instead of an insect.

Before Poorly Boy went on the defensive he sighed, running a hand wearily through his untidy hair.

"Mum always wants the fish from her favourite fish shop every time. Dad and Peter know they're much nicer from the village near where we go fishing. Little Sheeps thought Mr Brown and me could give the poorest pussy cats a good fish supper on the riverbank – sausage as well, seeing as it got in by mistake. Then we could get proper fish and chips – which we did, and took them home for our supper. That way, Mum really got to eat proper fish and chips – after she'd stopped sulking 'cos we didn't get sausage for her. And, this way, Mr Brown got to eat with us, because he paid for it all as I didn't have no money. Mum never usually invites him 'cos she says he's nearly as messy as I am at table. He's not at all – it's because Mum dun't like people to see that she has more to eat than the men do."

Poorly Boy was pleased to see Nelly's trunk relaxing. The threat seemed to have passed.

"That note under my bum – it doesn't explain why Uncle Peter and your dad didn't come after you, the stupid sheep and Mr Brown, who's old enough to know better. Why? Tell me or I'll trunk you!"

"All the note said was that we'd pinched the supper and wouldn't be back till later. After all, I'd been chucking things out of windows, re-flying dead butterflies and making sure Mum saw me, and telling her why I was doing it. She, like you – dafty! – thought I was going to bring her sausage back to life! In a way I did it by helping to keep the cats going. It's part of their life now – so it's kind of living on." He giggled, forgetting Nelly's trunk in his exuberance. He remembered it, and, as straight-faced as possible, said sorry for calling her 'dafty'. Then he went on with his story: "What Mum doesn't know is that Mr Brown phoned Uncle Peter on Thursday to tell him what Little Sheeps had planned for Friday. Uncle Peter told Dad, and, as both of them are as fed up with Mum's fish and chips as I am – but daren't tell her – they kept her calm until we came back. Dad said he'd tell us off when we did, and that made her happier."

"Rightly so," agreed Nelly. "Why didn't she, then?"

"Because she enjoyed the fish," smirked Poorly boy.

Nelly fixed him with a stern, thoughtful stare. "So this was all Little Sheeps' idea, was it?"

"Sort of," nodded Poorly Boy emphatically.

Nelly turned slowly towards the still-sulking sheep. He stopped rubbing his knee as she caught his attention with her trunk.

What?" he said. "You aren't?"

"I am," said Nelly.

A Good Turn Returned

A breeze, like a letter, slots in, no problem. Also, letter-like, a breeze can carry a problem. This particular breeze had problems and was slotting through the gap atop Poorly Boy's bedroom window one warm summer evening. Breezes are like ghosts and Canadian Mounted Police – when there's something on their mind, they always find a way to get through and get the job done.

Winds expect breezes to grow up fairly quickly and become useful citizens, doing things like filling yacht sails and helping birds and clouds get about. A mature breeze should be responsible enough to touch lovers' cheeks on evenings such as this – for only then can it be deemed responsible to graduate to young-wind status and get a job with prospects of becoming a wise, old, much respected wind in charge of tides and seasonal changes. This breeze had been a breeze too long and was grown childish (which is a vice) and no longer childlike (which is a virtue in breezes and people alike). The vice is what happens to breezes and people kicking leaves the autumns through, aimlessly wasting time.

But in the pond, the other morning, this breeze had seen its pointless face and wanted to move on. It had to prove it had a heart by doing something caring as a way to get the job it had in mind – a job it had seen advertised in those clouds above hills where such things are posted.

Poorly Boy awoke next morning in a most breezy state of mind.

"Mum, Uncle Peter's off fishing today. Do you fink he'll leave the fish to find something else to laugh at instead of at him trying to catch them and come wiv me 'n' Little Sheeps?"

"No," said Sue.

"Oh, go on – phone him. Tell him it's important enough for Little Sheeps to have a dream about it."

"Sure – that ought to do it." Sue couldn't help the sarcasm.

A light breeze touched her face through the open door from the kitchen.

"Well, OK, then," she relented – after all, her younger brother would only come home bad-tempered if he went – the fish were sure to laugh at him, as Poorly Boy put it.

"No," said Uncle Peter on his mobile. "My gear's packed and I'm off. Little Sheeps can tell his friend it's fish on the menu today, not favours."

Unaccountably, the old waterproof Uncle Peter took with him in case it rained slid off the chair back. Perhaps it was just a breeze through that window. He thought of his nephew's disappointment. Uncle Peter changed his mind.

They drove to the spot where the breeze recalled having played often with its mates. Such fun the three of them had had. All about the woods, fields and hills they'd spent those long-ago days together.

"So now what?" asked Uncle Peter as he sat beside Poorly Boy and Little Sheeps, the soft-toy lamb in Poorly Boy's hand.

It was warm, but a breeze tugged their hair impatiently, as if it wanted them to get on.

"Little Sheeps says go that way along that path 'n' he'll tell us where to go, Uncle Peter."

Uncle Peter squinted ahead through the windscreen in the direction Poorly Boy's finger indicated, and he ignored the urge to tell Little Sheeps where to go.

After the small group of trees came a sort of clearing. After this came a field, or fields, full of newly erected wind turbines.

They contemplated the soothing blades leisurely turning overhead.

"Not been up long these, Poorly Boy – only a few months or so."

"I don't know round here, Uncle Peter, but it's where Little Sheeps' friend was when he wanted him to turn his good around."

'How large Poorly Boy's eyes are!' thought Uncle Peter, not for the first time. 'What a curious way he has of putting things!'

The breeze nudged between them in the silence of Uncle Peter's meditation. Uncle Peter simply followed Poorly Boy's hand as it rose, Little Sheeps indicating the perimeter fence. At a rough level with Uncle Peter's eye was what appeared to be a ribbon – no, a thin leather strap with a small shiny disc attached. It was an identification tag – name, address and all that – probably found and placed there by a workman who couldn't be bothered to look into it further.

He was probably twenty or thereabouts, Uncle Peter guessed.

The young man forced a lukewarm smile on his otherwise cold exterior. He fingered the collar.

"It wasn't one of the greatest childhoods." He ran a quick hand through his hair, as if pushing those days backwards.

"Dad had, er, problems, let's say. We used to clear off to the country around, Wolf and me, leaving Mum and him to sort his moods out between them." His lips moved just as much as necessary from their naturally hard, straight line. "Dad cleared off when I was fifteen. I was out with mates and left Mum to it. Till she was ill, and eventually we lost her, she'd regularly take Wolf to those haunts of his puppy days. He was always dragging her there. The both of them seemed happy, the few times I noticed." The young man spoke in an emotionless monotone. Uncle Peter noted that he never took his eyes off Little Sheeps, who he could have sworn was actually glaring back. Uncle Peter hadn't had much occasion to ponder what sheep – real or soft toy – looked like when livid. He was grateful to the breeze on his face, which brought him back from feeling he was going mad.

In that moment it was over. The young man simply dropped the collar on the step, closed the door and left Poorly Boy, sheep in hand, and Uncle Peter standing there.

"So the old and sick dog took itself off to places it'd once been happy, knowing it was going to go to sleep there for ever

– unloved and lonely with the man's mother gone and him no doubt barely bothering with him."

Sue reflectively looked at her cup on the kitchen table, at which she sat with her son and brother.

"I remember that once a poor old dog came painfully alongside us with Little Sheeps in his mouth. It was just after Poorly Boy came out of hospital – one of his first trips in the buggy." She chuckled. "And boy, was it slow! I was so afraid something would happen to him – so fearful about his poorly heart – that for weeks I'd treat him like bone china! No wonder Wolf caught us up, even though he could barely walk."

Little Sheeps used Poorly Boy's finger to stroke some tears from below Sue's eyes.

"Wolf knew Little Sheeps' job was looking after me. I fell asleep and Wolf saw me drop him," said Poorly Boy.

"Funny name, Wolf, for a Labrador," observed Uncle Peter.

"Maybe the young man when he was a boy called him that because he hoped he'd eat his dad up," suggested Poorly Boy.

Uncle Peter returned and fastened the collar to the perimeter fence, the wind farm whirring busily away. He heard a dog bark not far off – a friendly, welcoming bark of recognition and warmth. It was evening – could be someone taking their dog out?

Poorly Boy's eyes opened. He was only dozing anyway. A gust of wind thumped the window with that gentle attention-grabbing thump some winds have.

"Pleased you're happy now and like your new job," said Poorly Boy, scrambling up from the pillow.

There was no other sound so he lay back.

"That man has no feelings." Little Sheeps spoke very close to Poorly Boy's nose on the pillow. "Turned into his dad, in fact – left his mum and Wolf behind, and now both are gone he couldn't care less! Didn't want the collar Wolf thought he might like to remember him by. But I tried – did the good turn for him by taking him to the man's house. Wolf knows who his friends are and where he stands, even if we're here and the man's mum and Wolf are invisible, doing a good job keeping the young wind company at the wind farm – lots of silver trees too, and a dog'll like that."

Poorly Boy continued to focus crossed eyes on Little Sheeps' small black nose. He wondered how his woolly chum had kept quite so long, and if he felt better for letting it all go. Poorly Boy didn't say anything, though. He just hoped that someday the young man would give over kicking leaves and go get another dog.

The Flea Of Them

"No! Higher, you idiot human boy!" fumed Little Sheeps.

"Mind my nose twerp!" replied the idiot human boy.

This may not be the most promising way to forge an atmosphere for working together. A heavy cloud of insults will not bring about the best of results when two are involved in a delicate, tedious and potentially dangerous task. Saying, "Me legs, me legs, you clout-minded sausage-slitting side plate!" is no way to avoid disaster. So when that disaster does come, in the form of a punch, the "Take that, fleece face! Don't you call me that what you just did again, neither!" which accompanies it is to be expected if not condoned.

At the best of times it is unwise to leave a five-year-old to jack up a car. If Little Sheeps is in charge, the one who left them to it is not only unwise, but not safe to be at large and should be locked up. Poorly Boy's father should have been much wiser.

"Your dad should be locked up, leaving us to do jacking with nothin' but a square handled screwdriver and a book end!" said Little Sheeps with some feeling.

"He only did it to shut me up," retorted a horizontal Poorly Boy, "'cos he was fed up wiv me having good ideas he didn't have."

"Get it up higher – will you, stupid? – or it'll slide off again," retorted Little Sheeps, retorting to Poorly Boy's retort.

Poorly Boy sat up on the Garden Shed Infirmary's floor in a sudden flurry of angry woodchips and sawdust. He plonked the screwdriver down and glared at Little Sheeps, who glared back.

"OK, know-it-all, you go round back and shove the bookend wiv the pot owl attached to it up its boot harder and I will get my finger in further so's I can!"

Poorly Boy was shouting so loudly that the car rolled off his finger, as Little Sheeps said it would.

Sometime later the two motor mechanics, or 'manacles' as Nelly insisted they were called, stood away beamingly, self satisfied, congratulating each other on a job well done and on how good the red cat collar looked around the midriff of the blue toy diecast car.

"Flea collar, I suppose," said Nelly from the onion bench.

"'Course." There was pride in Poorly Boy's voice.

"Now what?" enquired Nelly.

The beaming silence from the two car mechanics said it all; Nelly filled in the silly smiling vacancy with the incredulous words "Not the _ "

"Yes, the –" interrupted Poorly Boy and Little Sheeps in unison, themselves interrupted as they went off through the Garden Shed Infirmary's ever half-open door towards the garage.

There Ben, thoughtfully grim-faced, was wiping his hands on a cloth. Upon the fearsome twosome's arrival, Ben was still silent. He opened the door of the family car as if it had been prearranged, allowing Little Sheeps and Poorly Boy to crawl in between the driver's seat and the dashboard in order to strap, five–year-old-fumblingly, a nice shade of green flea collar around the steering column.

"That'll stop your car itching, Dad," said Poorly Boy.

His tongue returned inside his mouth after it came out to inspect the buckle on the collar. Ben returned to wiping his hands, slowly, absently, as his son and his son's best chum skipped, fleecy bottom in hand, back to the Garden Shed Infirmary.

Ben thought back to the previous evening, when Sue, sitting in the back of the car, had screamed and slapped her wrist. It seemed that the family cat, Felix, had left a friend of his in the car that morning after a routine visit to the vet. Little Sheeps and Poorly Boy, sitting beside Ben in the front, had gazed round as best they could, restrained in the safety harness, and Ben, glancing at their expressions, had had a not unfamiliar foreboding.

So when Little Sheeps had got Poorly Boy to explain his Little Sheeps' experiences of fleas in fields and cars and how to deal with them, Ben was not much surprised.

"They start off small, you see, Mum 'n' Dad," preached Poorly Boy from Little Sheeps' sermon notes. "Cats get 'em. They like cats, and cats like them. Then sometimes they get into cars and tractors – even army tanks and lorries, Dad, so watch it when you go to work."

Ben nodded at the caution, but he didn't think his lorry was likely to be threatened by either a flea, or a tank with a flea in command firing at him. Sue went on reading her fortune in the crystal ball of the sauce bottle's label.

"Anyway," continued Poorly Boy to the listless silence which seemed to him nowhere near enough engrossed, "Little Sheeps has first-hand-bite knowledge on what 'appens to fleas when you give them bright colours to play with. He read the book he wrote on it, see," added Poorly Boy, going over the top rather, irritated by his parents' seeming indifference. "They gather about the colours and stop there while you take them outside, where the cool air brings them round from being hypnotised by the colours. And yes – before you both ask, out of interest – the same simple meffod works just as well in fields. Ask yourself, why are cat collars coloured and why does sheep have them coloured blobs the farmer blobs on them? Now you've got it, haven't you? It's so the farmer can pick a sheep up and carry it outside the sheep field, through a gate, to someplace he dun't want fleas *not* to be, and then he brushes them off the paint patch. It's just exactly like you take the cat's collar outside and brush the fleas off it – no different."

Ben was beginning to scrub his shaving rash, while nodding simulated interest, on his elbow-propped knuckles; Poorly Boy's chin was happily wagging on his elbow-propped knuckles; and Mum's chin had found out what its future held in the sauce label. She got on with it by asking Poorly Boy how many he wanted.

"Two should do it, Mum: one collar for my new car and one for dad's old one. Felix is OK as the flea he had was his friend and now lives in Dad's car anyway. Anyway, Little Sheeps says cats never have more than one flea at a time; you just think there's more than one 'cos they move fast."

"Thank the great god of pork chops you never told them the truth!" said Little Sheeps as Poorly Boy's hand with Little Sheeps in it trotted with the both of them towards the Garden Shed Infirmary.

Inside Nelly was waiting in an alert-and-ready line on the onion bench with Daddy Springy, Baby Kenneth, and Mr Crumble Bee poised for inaction.

"Where's the flea?" they asked together.

"Won't be long," replied Poorly Boy.

"You lot's got to wait by the cottage-cheese carton and help Poorly Boy put the lid on when the one in Dad's car's been caught. Me 'n' Poorly Boy only told the grown-ups the half of it- we didn't want to frighten them, did we, Poorly Boy?"

Little Sheeps finished and Daddy Springy asked in an unbelieving voice if His Sheepfulness would go over it again.

Little Sheeps settled himself on the onion bench of his special moment's royal if smelly palace and wearily reiterated:

"Like I told you, fleas are born in batches of ten in mouse holes on fluff and dust. They grow a bit and find a cat – one flea, one cat only. It stays on the cat, quite harmless, just tickling it to make it laugh every now and then when the flea sees its buddy cat's being ripped apart by a dog, or else is having to wait for its tea. Trouble really starts if a flea gets in a car somehow or other, 'cos then it becomes angry, vicious, red-faced, moody and dangerous."

"Yes, Little Sheeps, as you told us earlier. That's because car drivers are all like that and fleas learn fast, right?"

"Right, Poorly Boy!" affirmed Little Sheeps. "In the end", he went on, "the flea gets that out of control in the small space of a car's insides that it goes off its rocker and up the wall."

"Oh my god, what language!" muttered Nelly.

Little Sheeps ignored her and pressed on regardless: "It eats the whole car, inside out, and swallows the driver, trainers 'n' everything."

"How come no one sees this – that's what I've been wondering since you told us this the first time?" Daddy Springy was doubting in his tone.

Little Sheeps sighed as if he thought any soft toy of Daddy Springy's supposed wisdom should have known without explanation. "Because the car disappears without trace, in an instant, into a very tiny black stomach that stretches a lot. All over in a second, it is," Little Sheeps clarified.

"Don't car drivers have family and friends who love them and miss them and report them missing?" Nelly asked, deeply concerned.

"No," said Little Sheeps, as if such a question was unbelievably stupid, even for Nelly. Undaunted, he ploughed on: "From cars, once they've got the taste for blood and exhaust gases, they go onto sheep, which the fleas find easier to digest then drivers. If you look carefully, and know what you're looking for, you can see all this happening. Watch a cat near a parked car. See the flea climb up on the bonnet and wait to get in when the door's opened – either that, or else it hangs about the hub caps, chases off after the wheels when the card drives away and jumps up to catch the exhaust pipe, first with its teeth and then with its muscular arms. Then it swings beneath the car, where it finds a crack to gain entry."

"Or waits till it stops and the door opens."

"That's right, Poorly Boy," confirms Little Sheeps. "Why," went on a fast talking fleece, "I've actually seen a flea chasing a cat, with another flea in front chasing a bus, with another in front of that chasing down a sheep – *and* all on the same road, *and* all at the same time , *and* all at once! Scary it was."

"And that's why we don't want to frighten Mum and Dad – frighten Mum especially – into slapping poor insolent car fleas when they's only just come off cats and dun't know the world and wouldn't itch a fly. Slap them, she does, upon their little bottoms so hard she could make them cry. And I'm not having *that* on my watch, as Uncle Peter says!" concluded the passionately indignant Poorly Boy.

"Come on!" urged Little Sheeps. "You lot talk too much. Let's get back to your dad, poorly Boy, and see if we can take the cat collar with the flea on it off the steering thingy. We'll run back here so's you mob on the onion bench, who talk so much, can talk flea into finding shelter and safety in the cottage-cheese tub, away from cruel mummies."

Just in time, Ben managed to complete vacuuming the car's interior. Poorly Boy wouldn't know and everyone could go on playing charades – or something far less polite, which Ben muttered under his breath just as Little Sheeps and Poorly Boy bounded into view.

That night with the flea safely asleep in its new home inside the Garden Shed Infirmary after being made to feel so welcome by the team and the lid of the cottage-cheese carton, Poorly Boy's tousled head of hair and ideas lay nestled in the cups of his hands on his pillow. From smiling happily up at the ceiling, he turned without rising to smile up at Little Sheeps on the bedside cabinet. The big moon, staring through the gap in the bedroom curtains, must have taken a shine to Poorly Boy's smile. Suddenly the smile vanished, but the moon seemed brighter as it grinned in at the darkening mood of the scene in the bedroom.

"You sure it's in there, aren't you, Little Sheeps?" enquired Poorly Boy.

"Course I am! I saw it go inside, frisky and gay as a spring lamb, only blacker, smaller and with more legs. Heck, I know a flea when I see one! I'm a sheep aren't I? Sheep can see things nothing else can!" said Little Sheeps with not a blink.

Poorly Boy was expressionless enough for even the moon to recognise the expression of the true unbeliever, but this brought forth from Little Sheeps, again, not a blink.

"You itch as well, don't you, Little Sheeps?" asked Poorly Boy, anxious and hopeful, rubbing his armpit athletically with the pillow whilst sitting up in bed.

"No," said Little Sheeps, quite without expression.

The In't Tit

Uncle Peter sighed and closed the book. Shadows were beginning to roost on the desk amongst the volumes there (some open, many closed), making a kind of terrain across which words settled for the night in thick, dark sentences and less dense clusters of lines.

The volumes had such titles as *British Birds, Birds of Britain, Rare and Even Rarer Birds of Britain, etc.*

"Are you thinking, Uncle Peter?"

Uncle Peter swivelled the chair (black plastic 'leather' – one of his rare indulgences) to face the chirruped question from behind. His nephew's eyes beamed with a brightness, brown and full of reading lamp.

"Who have you got to go with you? Our world's foremost sheep expert on birds, is it? Let's have a look," said Uncle Peter, relieved to be away from his irksome studies.

"Yes, it is him. How did you know Uncle?"

Poorly Boy sat on Uncle Peter's knee; Little Sheeps was jogging along there too.

"We could do with a hand and cloven hoof. The books describe what an osprey looks like, but not if we're likely to find one. They're rare and never seen in this area. Big bird of prey, it is. Can't think of what it can eat here, unless it's Little Sheeps."

Poorly Boy giggled and pretended to make the soft-toy sheep run up Uncle Peter's thigh and around his waist to hide round the back, out of the way of any osprey in the room. Little Sheeps peeped out from under Uncle Peter's arm.

"You know how good Little Sheeps is with birds, 'cos you told Mum so, Uncle. He knows every sparrow in our garden by name; and when each one's had enough beetles to fill his tummy, he tells them to clear off and not be greedy."

"Yes, I dare say," chuckled Uncle Peter. "Come on – let's have you and the great feather brain to bed. We need to be up with the worms to catch them on the wing – or something like that."

"Do worms fly, Uncle Peter?" came the small astonished voice.

Local sightings had begun some weeks previously. For a start, Coleman hadn't been much interested. It wasn't the rarest bird in the world a few locals were getting excited about. So what if an osprey had been seen in these parts? What was especially newsworthy about that, when there were robberies, scandals surrounding councillors and plans for new shopping malls to fill up and sell out the paper all the time with? But as lack of newsworthy subjects coincided with the persistence of these bird-sightings, Coleman decided, despite his own lack of interest, to get Uncle Peter to go and do some investigative journalism.

Whilst Uncle Peter was telling Sue about it on the phone, two little ears perched on either side of a tousled thicket on their owner's head were listening intently. Whenever the phone rang, Poorly Boy would pull at Sue's arm until she sat down so he didn't miss anything important he might be able to help with. In this case he could certainly be of assistance – or rather Little Sheeps could. Not that he said as much at the time – for now, all that mattered was persuading Sue and Uncle Peter to let him go bird-finding.

Sue put the phone down while fending off her son's protests firmly.

"No, you can't go. Uncle Peter's at work, not going out playing with you."

"But, Mum, Uncle Peter wants us to go with him 'cos he doesn't know nothing about birds. It's not fair, because Little Sheeps knows everything about them because his dad lived all his life in a field watching what they did."

"No – and I don't care," said Sue, firm as rams' horns.

Poorly Boy was so angry that he threw Little Sheeps on the floor; then he picked him up, cuddled him and started to cry because he'd hurt his beloved soft toy.

"Now look what you've done to him! You've upset him and made his tail bleed," he sobbed theatrically.

"Him? He's as tough as a thermal vest. And anyway, you threw him, not me."

The phone rang again:

"Sue, send him over. Let him come."

"No, he can't, Peter. He's been a naughty boy – flown into a tantrum and broken Little Sheeps' legs," she replied indignantly. "He's got to learn to do as he's told. I'm adamant he's not going bird-spotting tomorrow."

"It's not bird-spotting – it's searching for an osprey."

"Whatever it is, your nephew is not going!"

There was silence in the room and at the other end of the line.

"Mummy, out of the whole shed, Little Sheeps is the only one who can help Uncle. Even I couldn't tell him what Little Sheeps can," said Poorly Boy plaintively.

"Fine!" said Mum. "Uncle Peter can call and pick Little Sheeps up in the morning, and you can wave them off with the rest of the team from the shed."

"But he's right, Sue," came her brother's voice in her earpiece, fortunately for Poorly Boy only a phone's length away.

"Oh, come on – how green do you think I am!" she exclaimed defiantly, though beginning to sense defeat. "I know what's coming next," she said – which she did. "You're going to say Little Sheeps won't go with you unless Poorly Boy's with him, aren't you, Peter?"

Actually, with his sister guessing so astutely what was coming next, and with her sarcasm being quite unnecessary, he felt, he decided it was best not to say anything.

Thus – only because little Sheeps was good with birds, and Sue wasn't allowed by law to strangle her little brother (and under the circumstances it was probably as well her son was out of the house too) – Poorly Boy spent that evening and night at his uncle's, swotting up on birds from the white curly-nylon expert.

Poorly Boy phoned to say goodnight.

"Mum," he cooed, "I'm sorry Little Sheeps upset you. He's crying and won't go to sleep. Will you tell him you love him?"

Drily, to herself, Sue thought that if she knew Little Sheeps, he couldn't care less whether she was upset or not.

"Mummy," came the small, soft voice again, "please tell him you forgive us both."

Sue smiled broadly – Poorly Boy was not there to see it.

In bed that night, Little Sheeps was worried – though not about upsetting Sue.

"How are you going to get us out of this, then, Mr Smartie Smart?"

The white sheep with the pink face and sharp black eyes was staring at Poorly Boy nose to nose; they were so close on the pillow that Poorly Boy was looking cross-eyed.

"You only said I was a bird expert because you were playing with me when the phone rang. Just think: it could have been Baby Kenneth you're going bird-catching with!"

"He's too young and his brain's not big enough to learn things yet. Anyway, you're the one with the biggest head in the shed," observed Poorly Boy, whose eyes were hurting from crossing them too long. He blinked and told Little Sheeps to stand back a bit on the pillow. "In't it great, little Sheeps, to be looking for ostriches? I thought they lived in other places, not here, and I didn't know they dived for fish."

"I don't care where they live and I don't care if they go to the chip shop. What bothers me is I won't know one when I see it."

Poorly Boy, still staring into Little Sheeps' beady black eyes by the light of his Whisty Claypipe bedside lamp, thought about this.

"You will if he gets the chips wrapped," he said. "Anyway, they can't fly, so it's easy, in't it? Any bird not flying, or stood about waiting for a fish so's it can dive in after it, must be an ostrich."

"That's helpful." Little Sheeps thanked him. "What if it's a sparrow near a puddle, having a look round for a fly to catch for dinner?"

Poorly Boy thought once more.

"I think sparrows are smaller than ostriches," he offered.

"Stop mucking about," said Little Sheeps exasperatedly. "You don't know for sure that's the problem."

He got no further. His two brown eyes were roosting for sleep.

"I'm sorry I broke your legs," said Poorly Boy with a yawn.

An idea came to Little Sheeps: maybe, seeing as his legs were broken, neither he nor his vast absence of bird knowledge would be needed.

Over breakfast, Poorly Boy was distantly preoccupied. Looking out through the window, he gazed at the early sun, not too bright yet, or up and about, but still sat on the edge of the east, pulling this July morning on like a pair of yellow socks.

"I'm only thankful we've got Little Sheeps with us," said Uncle Peter, munching on his toast and marmalade. "Why is he laid on his side? Is he dead?" he continued cheerfully.

"His legs are broken, Uncle Peter."

"The lot?" Uncle Peter was astonished that he hadn't been told this the night before, though not astonished enough to stop munching. "I suppose that happened when you threw him on the floor in temper."

"Maybe a bit – but it wasn't me dropping him that did it really. It was that he fell when he got there on the floor."

"Do I detect a sullen note, Poorly Boy?" Uncle Peter said jauntily.

"No, Uncle Peter. His legs have always been thin."

Uncle Peter was waiting for his nephew to add 'honest' to this, but he didn't.

"Looks like we can't go, then. Suppose I ought to phone Coleman and tell him it's off as our bird expert's been injured."

Poorly Boy rose so quickly from his chair that Uncle Peter was certain his poorly heart would either give out or take off.

"No, Uncle Peter!" he exclaimed while righting his chair. "Mr Crumble Bee said he's got to be kept moving when his legs are broken as they heal faster that way."

Poorly Boy's pained grin reminded his uncle of a Hallowe'en pumpkin, for some odd reason. Uncle Peter loved to test Poorly Boy's inventive skills up to the edge – and then join him, so they both fell over together, laughing.

"Oh, I remember. That's quite correct: he did say that. I was visiting my Floppy Duck in the Garden Shed Infirmary when he had the nylon feathers chewed from his bum by that friend of mine's terrier. Little Sheeps had been caught stealing chocolate eggs from the toy chicken Jennifer brought in with hen's diabetes, and Jennifer stamped on Little Sheeps, so causing a compound fracture of his left rear fibia. Do you remember, poorly Boy?"

Poorly Boy was under the table, head from the eyes up peeping over the top as if wondering whether it was safe to come out. His eyes must have spoken, as the mouth wasn't visible.

"If your Floppy Duck goes with us, he can look after Little Sheeps; and he dun't mind travelling in cars, 'cos you found him at a car boot sale."

"And", continued Uncle Peter as if continuing the same sentence, "he knows about those birds of a bigger sort than visited Little Sheeps' father's field, or your garden."

The phone rang.

In the car, travelling to Lakeside Farm, Uncle Peter explained:

"While we were having our breakfast, my editor had a call from Mr McGregor, the farmer. That's where we're going now. He wanted to know if any reporter had been assigned to the osprey thing. My editor wants us to go and see what he's got to tell us about our rare bird of prey."

"He won't pray while we're there will he, Uncle? We prayed and sang hymns when little Kelly was given her name in church. Prayers are lovely, like poetry, but they always go with awful hymns."

Uncle Peter explained even further about ospreys and how they feed upon fish and how ospreys weren't ostriches. He'd mentioned this to Poorly Boy the night before, but Poorly Boy hadn't been listening. The page had been open at a big colourful ostrich and his ears were taken up with listening to his eyes gazing at that. Even now, in the car, Poorly Boy was only partly able to listen, Floppy Duck was being a poor nurse – the sort who'd sooner fight with a patient than tend one.

Engine off, Uncle Peter turned to Poorly Boy in the silence of bird call and July talking to its countryside.

"The feathers on Floppy Duck's bum never grew back, did they, Uncle Peter?" He was looking down, absently flicking Floppy Duck's tail. "Are you sure there's no ostriches round here?"

"Only on ostrich farms," said Uncle Peter.

"Can we go to one of them, then?"

"Not today, Come on, trooper – let's go."

With that Uncle Peter locked the car doors out of habit, and took off towards the white farmhouse. Poorly Boy walked at his heels along with Little Sheeps. Uncle Peter had to hold Floppy Duck to stop her fighting with Little Sheeps.

"It's not 'trooper'; it's 'space cadet'," said Poorly Boy. "Baby Kenneth started the space cadets, and I'm the boss of 'em."

Baby Kenneth had had a lifelong fascination with things to do with space, Peter knew. He also knew the best way to stop his nephew asking hopeless *cans* was to bring up his team and talk about them.

Alec McGregor's wife opened the door.

"And when he gets older he's going to take Nelly and me to that big planet named after the dog."

"Who is?" she asked.

"Baby Kenneth is," Poorly Boy said.

"It's a real dilemma – but we'll play along, don't worry."

Uncle Peter thanked Mrs McGregor and declined the third cup of tea. Poorly Boy was putting Little Sheeps' legs back on, after cutting them off when winning the battle they'd waged with two sword-handled brass pokers on the hearthrug during the last hour.

"If it got about we'd a nesting pair of ospreys in an outhouse, we'd have villains of every shape and size scaring them, the cattle and, ay," he chuckled Scottishly, "scaring Mavis and me as well!"

"Don't worry – I'll tell Coleman they're goshawks – been up the lake with you and seen 'em myself. I'll write a short column, with a big headline to the effect there's no rare birds in this vicinity. Before you know it, any villain wanting to pinch eggs will be back painting Coleman's car – again."

Mavis and Alec laughed and Uncle Peter refused the Scotch whisky once more. Poorly Boy did not refuse more cake. Floppy Duck, sitting on the table beside Uncle Peter, was obviously scared of the McGregor's dog and refused to move his golden beak.

"Ospreys are notoriously shy, so we can't risk getting near the nest site. Come on – I'll take you to a vantage point where we might get lucky. You can take a photo of it for the lad when he grows up."

Uncle Peter and Poorly Boy thanked Mrs McGregor, and Floppy Duck and Little Sheeps waved to her standing in the door way as Uncle Peter drove off after Farmer McGregor's truck.

Little Sheeps sat between Floppy Duck's legs on the slope of the sand dune they were sprawled behind.

"I can see right where Mr Alec is now sat with his tractor."

They'd been there some time, lying back in the sun, Uncle Peter chewing grass and sky-squinting from beneath his baseball cap.

"Can I lend these binoculars to Baby Kenneth for him to look at stars, Uncle Peter?"

Poorly Boy had happily been spying everything but the birds.

"When is Little Sheeps going to bird-spot for us?" Uncle Peter enquired mischievously.

There was no reply, apart from July still talking to its afternoon countryside. The light breeze backcombed Poorly Boy's hair. His attention was fixed on something to the left. Uncle Peter was oblivious, blue-sky spotting. He continued speaking to the clouds and talking to July.

"This is no good, Poorly Boy. We're going to have to do some work; maybe, as its birds of prey we're after, we could lure them with Little Sheeps and Floppy Duck."

There was still no small voice of reply. Uncle Peter noticed how loud July could shout in the unusual silence surrounding Poorly Boy. He turned suddenly to one side and his cap fell off.

"Uncle Peter, look at Farmer. He's got his binoculars just like me, only he's looking over there. If I give you mine and Baby Kenneth's binoculars, you can see two birds like gliders high above the trees."

Uncle Peter scrambled to his feet after first scrambling down the dune as he lost his footing in his haste to stand.

"Uncle Peter, isn't it—"

"Yes – isn't it, indeed!" yelled Uncle Peter, jumping a good goalkeeper's leap into the air and saving the rest of the words before they left Poorly Boy's mouth.

The beautiful elegant birds circled graceful English July circles as all five below looked on open-mouthed and golden-beaked.

"Look, Uncle." Whispered Poorly Boy, tugging at his uncle's T-shirt just as he was about to line up his camera. "Little Sheeps is telling Floppy Duck he knew they were praying birds as soon as he saw them. You can tell they're praying because they're so, so beautiful."

"And who needs hymns, eh, Poorly Boy!" added Uncle Peter.

He could never again think of the day without a fond smile and lump in his throat the size of the Grampians recalling his and Floppy Duck's afternoon bird-spotting with that most loveable and unique of British birds, the little tousle-headed in't tit – as well as Little Sheeps finding some ospreys for them.